PROMISES
Marie Sexton

Published by
Dreamspinner Press
4760 Preston Road
Suite 244-149
Frisco, TX 75034
http://www.dreamspinnerpress.com/

Promises

Cover Art by Anne Cain   annecain.art@gmail.com
Cover Design by Mara McKennen

ISBN: 978-1-61581-378-0

Printed in the United States of America
First Edition
January, 2010

eBook edition available
eBook ISBN: 978-1-61581-379-7

Many thanks to—

My husband Sean,
for his unwavering love and
support, even when I was completely
obsessive and monopolized the computer.

Carol Ibanez, whose guidance
helped me turn a novella into a novel.

Amy Caroline, my greatest cheerleader
and sounding board, for reading every
version of this story, every deleted scene, and
every half-baked idea that drifted through my head.

This book is for the three of you,
without whom it would never have existed.

CHAPTER 1

THE whole thing started because of Lizzy's Jeep. If it hadn't been for that, I might not have met Matt. And maybe he wouldn't have felt the need to prove himself. And maybe nobody would have been hurt.

But I'm getting ahead of myself. Like I said, it started with Lizzy's Jeep. Lizzy is the wife of my brother Brian, and they were expecting their first child in the fall. She decided that her old Wrangler, which she'd had since college, just wasn't going to cut it as a family vehicle. So she parked it out front of our shop with a handwritten For Sale sign in the window.

The shop was started by my grandpa. Originally it was a hardware store, but at some point, auto parts had been added as well. When my grandpa died, my dad took over the store, and when he died, it passed to Brian, Lizzy, and me.

It was a gorgeous spring day in Colorado, and I was sitting with my feet up on the counter, wishing I was outside enjoying the sunshine, when he came in. He definitely caught my attention right away, simply because he wasn't from around here. I've lived in Coda my whole life, not counting the five years I spent in Fort Collins, at the university, and I knew everybody in town. So he was either visiting somebody in the area or just passing through. We're not a tourist town, but people do bump into us occasionally, either

1

looking for four-wheel drive trails or on their way to one of the dude ranches that are farther up the road.

He certainly didn't look like one of the middle-aged suckers who frequented the dude ranches. He was probably in his early thirties. He was taller than me by two or three inches, putting him just over six feet tall, with military-short black hair and a couple of days' worth of dark stubble on his cheeks. He was wearing jeans and a plain black T-shirt and cowboy boots. Broad shoulders and big arms showed he worked out. He was gorgeous.

"That Jeep run?" His voice was deep with a little bit of a drawl. Not Deep South drawl, but the vowels were a little longer than a Coloradoan.

"You bet. It runs great."

"Hmmm." He was looking out the window at it. "Why you selling it?"

"Not me. My sister-in-law. She says it'll be too hard to get a car seat in the back. She bought a Cherokee instead."

He looked a little confused by that, which told me he didn't have kids himself. "So it drives okay?"

"Perfect. Want to try it out? I've got the keys right here."

His eyebrows went up. "Sure! You need collateral or something? I can leave my license."

I think at that point, he could have talked me into about anything. My knees were feeling a little wobbly. I was trying to determine if I really was seeing a touch of green in those steel-gray eyes. I hoped I sounded casual when I said, "I'll go with you. I know the roads around here. We can take it up one of the easy trails so you can see how it handles."

"What about the store? Hate to leave you short-handed during rush hour." He raised an eyebrow toward the empty store, one corner of his mouth barely twitching up. "Won't your boss be mad if you leave?"

I laughed. "I'm one of the owners, so I can slack off if I want to." I turned and called into the back room, "Ringo!"

Our one employee came warily out of the back. He was always skittish with me, and if Lizzy wasn't around, he made a point of keeping his distance. I think he was expecting me to make a pass at him. He was seventeen, had stringy black hair, bad skin, and probably weighed a buck five soaking wet. I didn't have the heart to tell him that he wasn't my type.

"Yeah?"

"Hold the fort. I'll be back in an hour or so." I turned back to my tall, dark stranger. "Let's go!"

Once we were in the Jeep, he held his right hand out to me. "I'm Matt Richards."

"Jared Thomas." His grip was strong, but he wasn't one of those guys who had to break your hand to prove how macho he is.

"Which way?"

"Turn left. We'll just drive up to the Rock."

"What's that?"

"What it sounds like—a big fucking rock. It's nothing spectacular. People go up there to picnic. And of course, the teenagers go there sometimes to park or to get high."

He frowned a little at that. I was starting to think he didn't smile much. I, on the other hand, knew I was grinning ear to ear. Getting out of the store for a few minutes, especially to head into the mountains, was enough to brighten my day considerably. Doing it in the company of the best-looking guy I had seen in a hell of a long time sure didn't hurt either.

"So what brings you to our fine metropolis?" I asked him.

"I just moved here."

3

"Really? Why in the world would you want to do that?"

"Why not?" His tone was bantering, although his face was still serious. "You live here, don't you? Is it that bad?"

"Well, no. I love it here. That's why I've never left. But, you know, the town is dying. More people moving out than moving in. Towns along the front range are booming, but nobody wants to live up here and commute."

"I was just hired by the Coda PD."

"You're a cop?"

He raised an eyebrow at me and said with some amusement, "Is that a problem?"

"Well, no, but I wish I hadn't told you about the kids coming up here to get high."

He raised his eyebrow at me again and said lightly, "Don't worry. I won't tell them you're the rat." The good officer wasn't completely without humor. "So, you've lived here your whole life?" He didn't sound curious so much as like he was just trying to make casual conversation.

"Yep. Except for the years I spent in college."

"And you own the store?"

"Me and my brother and his wife, yeah. It's not a big money maker or anything, but we manage. Brian's an accountant, and he has other clients, so he mostly just does the books. Lizzy and I run the shop."

"But you went to college?" Now he sounded genuinely curious.

"Yeah, I went to Colorado State. I have a degree in physics and my teacher's certificate."

"Why aren't you a teacher?"

4

"I didn't want to let Brian and Lizzy down." That wasn't entirely true, but I didn't want to tell him the real reason: that I didn't want to deal with the fallout of being a gay high school teacher in a small town. "There isn't really anyone else to cover the shop. We can't afford a full-time employee. Well, we could if they didn't want benefits, but they do. So instead, we just have Ringo, part time. We get half his salary back, 'cause he spends his paychecks on stuff for his car, so it works out okay." I laughed. "Ringo! That can't be his real name." I realized I was babbling. "Sorry I'm talking so much. I'm sure I'm boring you."

He looked right at me and said seriously, "Not at all."

We had reached the end of the trail. "You'll have to turn around here."

He stopped the Jeep and looked around suspiciously. There were no other cars. "I don't see any rock."

"Just up the trail a bit. Want to walk up there?"

His face brightened a little at that. "You bet."

So we walked down the trail, through Ponderosa pines and Douglas firs and aspens that were just starting to bud to one of the rocky abutments that must have helped give the Rockies their name. The Colorado mountains are full of these giant piles of stationary rock, rounded and covered with dry sage- and rust-colored lichen. This one was about twenty feet high on the downhill side. If you walked up the hill, you could practically walk right out onto it. But what's the fun in that? Those rocks just beg to be climbed.

Once we reached the top, we sat down. The view wasn't really any different from there. We could see down the trail to the Jeep, but other than that, we were still just looking at more trees, more rocks, more mountains. I love Colorado, but this type of view can be found in hundreds of spots. I was surprised to hear a contented sigh from Matt. When I looked at him, his face showed amazement.

"Man, I love Colorado. I'm from Oklahoma. This is better,

believe me."

He turned to look at me, and I almost quit breathing. He was squinting a little against the sun. His skin was tan, and his eyes were shining. There was definitely a hint of green in them. "Thanks for bringing me up here."

"Anytime." And I meant it.

CHAPTER 2

MATT came by the shop the next day, cash in hand, to buy the Jeep. It was a Saturday, normally one of our busier days, so Lizzy and I were both in the shop.

"Will you join me for a beer?" He had shaved that morning, and it made him look several years younger. Man, he was cute.

"I'd love to, but you'll have to give me a rain check. I'm having dinner with the family."

"Oh." He actually sounded disappointed. "Well, maybe another time...."

"Hey!" Lizzy interrupted, grinning ear to ear. "Why don't you come? We're just having dinner up at the house. We would love to have you."

He agreed, and we arranged for him to come back by the shop shortly after we closed at five.

Once he was gone, I studiously tried not to look at Lizzy, who was standing next to me with the goofiest smile I'd seen in a long time. She has blonde hair that seems to fly all over the place when she moves and blue eyes, which at the moment were shining with excitement. I suppose she falls somewhere between "lovely" and "cute as a button," and I swear she could charm the stars down out of the sky if she tried.

"Well?" she finally asked.

"Well, what?" I knew I was blushing and hated myself for it.

"You know what." She smacked me on the arm. "He's hot! And he asked you out. Aren't you excited?" The fact was, I didn't have many friends. Most of my buddies from high school were married with kids. The ones who weren't married were all troublemakers who spent their nights drinking at the bar. Lizzy was probably the best friend I had in the world, and I knew that she was always hoping I would find somebody.

"I don't think he meant it as a date."

Her smile faltered a little. "You don't?"

"Does he look gay to you?"

"Well, no. But neither do you, so that obviously doesn't mean anything and you know it. He wanted to take you out and was disappointed that he wasn't going to have you alone. I think he's interested." The smile was back in its full glory now.

I felt a grin breaking out on my face. "I'm not going to get my hopes up, but I sure wouldn't mind if you were right."

PEOPLE always ask me when I knew that I was gay. I guess they think I had some epiphany—lights flashing and horns blaring—but it wasn't like that for me. It was more of a culmination of events.

I suppose the first clues came early in puberty as I compared myself to my brother Brian, two years my elder. While he was hanging up posters of Cindy Crawford and Samantha Fox, I was putting up only cars and the Denver Broncos. I was aware of the fact that he found girls enticing and fascinating in a way I did not understand, but I didn't think too much of it.

8

One weekend when I was fifteen, my dad went to a Broncos game and brought a poster back for me that showed the whole team with the cheerleaders arrayed around them in various provocative poses. Brian helped me hang it up, and then we stood there for a few minutes looking at it.

"Which one do you think is the best looking?" Brian asked me.

"Steve Atwater," I said without even thinking about it.

He laughed, but it was a nervous kind of laugh, like he wasn't sure if I was pulling his leg or not. When I turned to look at him, I found him staring at me with a look on his face that would eventually become very familiar to me: part humor, part confusion, part concern. I was embarrassed. I knew my answer was wrong, and yet, I wasn't really sure why.

"No," he said, "I meant which one of the *cheerleaders*?" In truth, I had barely noticed them.

Soon my friends were swapping skin magazines with shaking hands and boastful laughs. I wasn't exactly sure what they felt when they looked at them, but it was pretty clear it wasn't the same as the mild embarrassment I was feeling.

It wasn't until I met Tom that I realized exactly how different I was. Tom played football with my brother Brian. They were best friends. I was sixteen; they were eighteen. From the moment he walked in our front door behind my brother, I was infatuated with him. I could barely speak to him but couldn't keep my eyes off him. His laugh was enough to elicit physical responses that caused me to always have a school book in my hand when he was in the house— not because I was such a good student, but because I needed to be able to cover myself quickly. I walked a fine line between wanting to see him as much as possible and wanting to stay out of his sight. I knew Brian was watching me again with the same looks he had given me the day I blurted out Steve Atwater's name: concern, bemusement, embarrassment. It was something of a relief when the two of them finally graduated and went off to college.

9

After that, I was pretty sure, although I never said anything to anybody. I faked my way through high school. I never tried out for football because I was afraid of the complications that could arise in the locker room, if only in my imagination. I had a few dates with girls, but they were mostly group dates; we held hands a few times and a couple of them even kissed me. The kisses were, for me at least, completely uninspiring, bordering on disturbing, and it never went further than that.

Once I made it to college, away from home, I finally allowed myself to experiment. I met guys at the club or at the gym and had a few brief but meaningless affairs. Never found anything I would have called love, but I knew after that, without a doubt, that I was gay.

Needless to say, I never planned to be in my thirties and still alone. And being gay in a town this small isn't easy. Colorado isn't exactly a gay Mecca; it's not the Bible belt, but it's not San Francisco either. Most of the town knows about me, and most of them even accept me, but a few still look the other way when I pass them in the grocery store or refuse to deal with me when they come into the shop. Chances of finding a partner in Coda were almost nonexistent, and chances of me ending up alone seemed depressingly high.

CHAPTER 3

SO THAT night, Matt met my family. Lizzy went home from work early, ostensibly to get a head start on dinner, but I think the real reason was so she could fill in Brian and Mom before we arrived. Brian, of course, was courteous. Mom was sizing him up but seemed to approve.

"Are you into mountain biking too?" she asked him at one point.

"I sold my bike before I moved here. I liked riding, but in Oklahoma, there aren't really any mountains to bike in. Why?"

"Jared's up there every time he has a day off. He goes alone. I keep telling him he shouldn't. What if he got hurt?"

"Mom, cool it. Have I ever been hurt?"

"You get hurt every time!"

Oh boy, here we go. I was resisting the urge to roll my eyes at her. "Mom, bumps and bruises don't count."

"But you don't even wear a helmet!"

She was starting to whine now. I hate the guilt trip, but I hate helmets more. "I do if it's a hard trail. I wish you wouldn't worry about it so much."

11

"But there's nobody with you, in case you need help."

"Talk to your other son, Mom," I said teasingly. "He's the one who won't ride with me anymore."

"I can't keep up!" Brian said, throwing his hands up like he was surrendering.

"Anyway," Lizzy cut in, "it's not the trails I worry about. It's here in town that scares me. Crazy drivers talking on their cell phones and never watching where they're going." She was shaking her finger in my direction. It was not the first time I had heard that speech. "You ride to and from work every day, and you never wear your helmet. It's not safe. I bet Matt can tell you about all kinds of terrible accidents involving bicyclists who weren't wearing helmets, right Matt?"

He looked amused. "I know better than to get in the middle of a family argument."

"Brian," I entreated, "save me from your wife!"

Brian laughed but took pity on me and changed the subject. "So Matt, are you a football fan?"

"Of course."

"You're from Oklahoma? Are you a Cowboys fan?"

He actually grinned a little, and I could tell he was getting ready to let some big cat out of the bag. "I'm a Chiefs fan."

"Oh no!" The whole table erupted. Lizzy started throwing rolls at him. We are a hardcore Broncos family, and declaring allegiance for our division rival, the Chiefs, was tantamount to heresy in our household.

Brian yelled gleefully, "Jared, you know better than to bring a Chiefs fan into my house! I should throw both of you out on your asses!"

"And you seemed like such a nice boy too," Mom said

12

mournfully but with a twinkle in her eye.

I was laughing. "Hey, I didn't know! I assumed anybody smart enough to live in Colorado would know who the better team was!"

"All right," Matt said. "Everybody calm down. You Broncos fans are so high strung!" That got him another round of razzing, and Lizzy threw another roll at him. He saw it coming, caught it, and turned to throw it at me. "You know, it could be worse. At least I'm not a Raiders fan!" And of course we all had to agree on that.

Right after dinner, Mom went home. I sent Matt out onto the patio while I went to fetch beer from the kitchen. When I walked in, Lizzy was beaming at me.

I tried to ignore that look and asked, "You coming outside with us?"

"Sure," Brian started to say, "as soon as—"

"No!" Lizzy cut him off, slapping his arm playfully. "No. We're going to give you boys some time alone."

"Ah." Brian looked a little troubled by that. I had a sudden Steve Atwater flashback. Obviously, knowing I was gay was one thing, but this was the first time he had ever really had to think about me with a potential suitor. I hadn't ever had a boyfriend serious enough to introduce to my family.

"Lizzy, I don't think that's necessary. I'm pretty sure that's not what he has in mind."

"I wouldn't be so sure. You two couldn't take your eyes off each other all through dinner. I'll just go upstairs, and Brian will clean up."

"What am I supposed to tell him?"

"Are you kidding? Tell him the pregnant lady got tired and had to lie down. It's not even a lie. I'm exhausted. But"—and she pointed a finger right at me—"I expect a full report in the morning."

Two beers later, I was feeling completely relaxed. We were sprawled in patio chairs, enjoying the unseasonably warm evening.

"So, are you married?" I asked him.

"Nope."

"Divorced?"

"Nope."

"Ever come close?"

"No."

Well, that seemed odd. At our age, I would at least have expected a near miss. Unless....

"Why not?"

He was starting to look uncomfortable now, fidgeting with the label on his beer bottle. "Guess I just haven't found a girl I felt that way about."

"What about a guy?" it was out of my mouth before my good sense could stop it. And, of course, I really did want to know.

"What? No!" He looked alarmed and a little big angry. "Of course not. Why would you ask that?"

That tiny flicker of hope that Lizzy had lit within me died. "It was just a question. It's no big deal. Sorry I brought it up."

"I'm not gay!"

"Okay."

"Why?" It sounded like a challenge. "Are you?"

"Yes." He would have found out soon enough anyway.

He was taken aback. He frowned at me, looked me up and down. "You are? I mean, I was kidding. I didn't really think that you would say yes."

14

I laughed uncomfortably. "Well, I am." I looked him square in the eyes. "Is that a problem?"

"Well…." To his credit, he actually stopped and thought about it. He was fidgeting with the label on his bottle again. "I don't know. I never…." The label came off, and he seemed confused about what to do with it now that it was free.

"You know, it's not contagious." I was teasing now and hoping he would realize it. But I was also pretty sure he wouldn't be asking me out for dinner or beers anymore.

"I know. Of course I know." He sighed, and his shoulders relaxed a little. He shook his head. "I'm being an ass. It's none of my business who you sleep with." A pause, and then, "Just, I want you to know"—his eyes were on mine again—"I'm not."

I smiled. "Hey, I'm not gonna kiss you or anything." Although the thought of doing exactly that was enough to make my pulse speed up a little. But it was apparently what he needed to hear, because he relaxed the rest of the way with a sigh. "Anyway, no self-respecting Coloradoan would date a Chiefs fan." That made him laugh, and after that, we were back on safe ground. The conversation seemed to be forgotten.

LIZZY called me first thing in the morning. "Well? What happened?"

"He's straight."

"Oh." She sounded as disappointed as I was. "Are you sure?"

"He was pretty adamant about it."

"Oh, Jared," she said sincerely. "I'm so sorry!"

"Lizzy, it's okay. Really. I barely know the guy. It's not like I'm in love with him or anything."

"I know, but you were so happy last night. I just want you to be happy."

"I know, Lizzy. I'm not gonna say I wasn't hoping. But he's straight, and I guess that's the end of it. I think I'll live."

CHAPTER 4

"GET a haircut already, you friggin' bum!" Lizzy was harassing me about my hair again. It was one of her favorite topics. "Really, Jarhead, whatever that look is, it's out."

I'm not a Marine. Lizzy finds it amusing to call me "Jarhead" instead of Jared any time she thinks I'm being particularly obtuse. Which is often.

The length of my hair is one of her favorite things to razz me about. The truth is that haircuts present something of a problem for me. There are only two places in Coda to get a haircut. There's Gerri's Barber Shop, where most of the men in town go. But Gerri is old school, one of the few people in town who treat me like I'm a pariah, so I can't go there. Then there's Sally's, the beauty salon that most of the women go to. I had been there a couple of times, but it was miserable. The girls seemed to think that me being gay meant that I wanted to gossip with them about who was sleeping with whom or debate the merits of Brad Pitt over Johnny Depp (neither is exactly my type). Once, I let Lizzy cut it, but that was a disaster that neither of us wanted to repeat.

My dark blonde hair is thick and coarse and naturally curly. If it's too short, I end up with curls sticking out every which way. But, if I let it grow, the curls at least hang down. I could have shaved it, but that seemed like too much maintenance. So what I end up with is

17

a wild mass of curls. Even I have to admit that it bears more than a passing resemblance to an old-fashioned mop. I try to tie it back when we're at the shop; if I pull the curls straight, it's just barely long enough to reach the rubber band. But by the end of the day, half of it will have escaped.

"Lizzy, I like being shaggy. This way you and I match, see?"

Her hair is about the same color as mine but longer, and her curls are more like soft waves. She flipped it over her shoulder and gave me the finger and then turned to Ringo.

"Ringo, tell Jared he needs a haircut!"

Ringo looked up in alarm from his schoolwork on the counter. Lizzy let him work on homework as long as we didn't have customers. "What? Are you talking to me?"

She rolled her eyes good naturedly. "Honestly! *Nobody* listens to me. What's got you so perplexed over there?"

"Advanced algebra." He threw his pencil down on his book and pushed his hair back off of his face with both hands. "How can anybody do this stuff?"

"You'll figure it out," Lizzy assured him.

"How? I don't understand any of it. My teacher just follows the book. My parents can't help me. Nobody can explain it to me in a way that makes sense." He picked his pencil back up and put his head in his hand as he bent back to his task. "I hate it!"

"Jared can help you."

"What?" Ringo and I exclaimed in unison. I was horrified that she would suggest it, and he obviously was, too, judging by the look on his face.

"Jared's really good at math. He's supposed to be a physics teacher, aren't you?" She gave me a piercing gaze, which I turned away from. "Maybe he can tutor you."

18

"Maybe." Ringo looked pretty skeptical. I didn't say anything.

Lizzy left shortly afterward since she had opened the shop that day. We didn't have many customers that afternoon, and Ringo spent most of his time trying to puzzle out his math problems. There was a lot of erasing going on, and I could tell he was getting frustrated. Every once in a while, he would glance up at me, and I knew he was debating whether or not to ask for help. I ignored him.

Finally, as I was closing out the register, he said hesitantly, "Jared, you really know how to do this stuff?"

"I really do."

"What did she mean, you're 'supposed to be' a teacher?"

"That's what I planned to do when I went to college."

"So why didn't you?"

I could have given him the same answer I had given Matt, but for some reason, I told him the truth. "The same reason you don't want me to tutor you. Some people think that just because I'm gay, I'm going to molest every young boy that crosses my path."

He was quiet for a minute, and I could tell I had embarrassed him. I felt a little bad about it, but I couldn't exactly take it back.

"That's what my dad says." His cheeks were bright red, and he wouldn't look at me. "He says I shouldn't be alone in the shop with you. I tell him Lizzy's always here. He doesn't know that she leaves sometimes."

My hands were shaking a little, and I was trying to control the urge to slam things around. "I'll be sure to keep my distance then."

"The thing is, you've never tried anything with me. I've never seen you hit on anybody."

"Kid, I'm gay. I'm not a pervert, and I'm not a pedophile."

"I'm not a kid," he said indignantly.

19

I took a deep breath to calm myself down. Of course, being seventeen, he didn't feel like a kid, even if he seemed like one to me. "I know. I'm just saying, just because I'm gay doesn't mean that I can't control myself. Or that I don't have standards. Do you hit on every single girl you see? Even the ones that are only fourteen? Or the ones that are dating other people?" Well, he had just turned seventeen; so maybe that was a bad example. "What about Lizzy? She likes men, too, but you don't worry about her making a move on you." I actually saw the wheels turning then as he thought about that. But I didn't want to talk about it anymore. Either he would figure it out or he wouldn't, but I didn't feel like staying on the soapbox. "Forget it, Ringo. I'm locking the doors. Turn the lights off when you leave."

"Jared, wait!"

I turned around. He was chewing on his lip, tapping his pencil nervously against his book, but at least he was looking at me. "I'm never going to pass this class without help. I can't pay you, but I'll work off the clock if you'll tutor me."

"What about your dad?"

He shrugged a little. "He wants me to pass. I'll work it out."

His sudden change in attitude surprised me. Maybe I really had gotten through to him a little bit. Or maybe he was really that desperate to pass. Either way, I was also surprised to find that the idea of tutoring him wasn't as dreadful as I had thought at first. I was actually looking forward to having something different to do. It might even be fun.

Fun?

That was a pretty sad indication as to the state of my social life. Still, sitting at a counter in a hardware/auto parts store wasn't exactly stimulating. At least this would exercise some of my neglected gray matter. I could almost feel those unused parts of my brain waking up, stretching, and looking around to see what was going on.

Ringo was still looking at me, waiting for my answer. Why not?

"Okay, kid. Let's see where you're at."

CHAPTER 5

RINGO turned out to be a good student. He had the bad habit of wanting to plug numbers into equations right away instead of working with the variables, but once I broke him of that, he started to make progress. He was also hindered a little by his pride. He often told me that he understood things before he really did, but he never gave up. I had been working with him for a couple of weeks when Matt showed up at the shop.

"Hi Jared!" he said as he came in. "I was hoping to catch you before you left." I hadn't seen him since that night at Lizzy's when he found out I was gay. I hadn't expected to hear from him again.

Lizzy immediately feigned great interest in a shelf of oil filters. I knew she was listening to every word but trying to look like she wasn't.

"I still owe you dinner and a beer. How about it?" He glanced around at Lizzy. "You're welcome to join us, of course."

"What? Me?" She managed to look flustered and embarrassed about being caught listening. "No. Brian's waiting for me, and I can't drink until after the baby's born. You two will have more fun without me."

We walked down the street to Mamacita's, our one and only Mexican restaurant.

"Are you sure you're okay with this?" I asked him before we went inside.

"Okay with what?"

"This is a small town. People will see you with me, and they'll make assumptions."

He frowned a little at that, and I realized it hadn't occurred to him. But then he shrugged. "It's just dinner."

"Okay. Don't say I didn't warn you."

Once we were seated, our waitress, Cherie, came over. "Jared, who's your friend?" she asked. Cherie and I went to school together from kindergarten all the way through high school graduation. Back then, she was gorgeous—blonde hair, brown eyes, curves in all the right places. She still is, I guess, but life has taken its toll. Some of the shine is gone, but she hasn't totally lost it. She's been married and divorced twice, both times to Dan, one of our local lowlifes. The rumors are that Dan liked to beat her up when he had been drinking, which was most of the time. She had even ended up in the hospital once. She at least had been smart enough to divorce him. Twice. And they didn't have any kids, which I thought was a blessing.

"Cherie, this is Matt. He's Coda's newest police officer." I was thinking about how Matt would undoubtedly be familiar with her ex-husband before too long. He was always getting in trouble for something. "Matt, this is Cherie. She's..." Trouble? Desperate? Lonely? "An old friend," I finished lamely.

"So glad to meet you!" She was practically batting her eyelashes at him. Somehow, I knew we were going to get great service while we were there.

He was definitely checking her out as she walked away. "So," he said, once she was gone, "did you and she date?"

I laughed. "No."

"Did you ever date any girls at all?"

23

Oh no. Not this conversation. Why did it always come down to this?

"No. I never seriously dated any girls."

"So, you've never…?" He let the question trail off, but it was obvious what he meant.

"No. Never with a girl."

"Well, how do you know—?"

I couldn't stop from rolling my eyes. "I just know. The fact that I've never even wanted to is a pretty big clue."

Cherie showed up with our drinks, beaming at him. He didn't seem to notice. When she was gone again, he said, "I'm sorry. It's none of my business."

"No worries. People often think that if we just try it, maybe we'll like it. But for me at least, it's not like that."

"For some, though?"

"I don't know. Obviously there are guys who like men but who still manage to get married and have kids. It must be different for them. I can't really say. I only know that I've never wanted to try. Women just don't appeal to me."

"Interesting." He was blushing a little. "What about, you know, the religious implications?"

"Are you asking me if I think it's a sin?"

"I guess so, yeah."

"I don't believe in God, so no. Once you take him out of the equation, it becomes a simple matter of consenting adults."

I could tell right away that made him uncomfortable.

"So you don't believe in God at all?" He didn't sound offended by the idea, just surprised.

24

"Not really. I just wasn't raised that way. My dad was an atheist. My mom, well, I guess you could call her a spiritual agnostic with Buddhist inclinations, if you know what I mean." The look on his face told me that he didn't. "I guess I figure there may be something out there that's godlike. Something we can't even begin to comprehend. But I can't imagine that he, or it, cares much who's in my bed." He didn't seem to disagree so much as to just be completely baffled. "I take it you're Christian?"

"I guess so. I don't know. I'm not a Bible thumper or anything, but I guess I've always believed that it must be true. My family's Baptist. Didn't go to church that often but always said grace before dinner. That kind of thing. I just never really thought about it much. How can so many people believe it if it's wrong?"

"The number of people who believe a thing has no bearing upon its truth."

He was still thinking about that when Cherie brought our food. "Need anything else, honey?" She didn't even look at me. He ordered two more beers.

I figured turnabout was fair play. "So how about you? You never felt attracted to another guy?"

His cheeks turned bright red, and the result was beautiful. "No, absolutely not." But it sounded like a lie to me. It was a little too quick and too harshly stated. In my experience, men who are truly straight don't have to defend themselves so obstinately.

"It's okay, you know? It's okay to admit that you're sometimes attracted to men. It doesn't mean that you're any less of one."

"No!" Not angry but a little annoyed.

"Okay. Did you play any sports in high school?" That might have sounded like I was letting him off the hook, but I wasn't through yet.

25

"I wrestled."

Perfect! Of course, now I was trying to picture him in one of those tight little leotard things that wrestlers wear.

"And when you were wrestling, rolling around on the floor with another guy, you never started to get turned on?"

"That's not the same."

That surprised me, actually. I had been expecting denial. "It isn't?"

"No. Everybody had that happen from time to time. It didn't mean anything. We're all wearing cups, so it's not like the other guy knows. I just, you know, thought about baseball or something until the problem resolved itself." He was recovering a little now, getting back to his usual bantering tone.

"Did thinking about baseball players make it go away?" I was grinning then, and I'm sure he knew I was teasing.

"Maybe not, but thinking about having the rest of the team kick my ass generally did the trick."

"Yes, I suppose it would."

We finished dinner and headed back to the shop. Despite the awkward topic over dinner, we lapsed easily back into comfortable conversation.

"So why did you become a cop?"

"Seemed like the thing to do. Do my duty. Protect and serve. God and country. All that happy horse shit."

"God and country? Are you a Marine or something?"

He frowned again. I was really wishing he would smile more. I was betting that his smile would be amazing. "No. My dad was, though. I was supposed to be. I don't think he's ever forgiven me for not enlisting. I joined the ROTC, but that wasn't really enough for him. Everyone else—my dad, my uncle, my grandpa—they were all military. I don't think they could ever understand why I didn't want that life. As far as he's concerned, it was my duty, and I failed."

Boy, did that explain a lot! He was looking embarrassed now, and I had the distinct impression he hadn't really meant to tell me all that. I wasn't surprised when he suddenly changed the subject.

"You ever gone geo-caching?" he asked.

"Nope. I've heard about it, but I don't have a GPS."

"I thought I would give it a shot next weekend. Want to join me?"

"Sure." I was trying to tell myself that this was not a date. Just buddies. And it would be nice to have a buddy, to be honest. Lizzy and Brian were great, but I was still lonely a lot. The idea of having a friend to hang out with was nice. I figured I better take advantage of it before one of the eligible women in town started monopolizing his free time. "That sounds like fun."

"Great! I'll pick you up at ten on Saturday." I was sure Lizzy wouldn't mind if I took the day off.

I gave him directions to my house and spent the rest of the week counting down the hours, cursing myself for a fool the entire time.

CHAPTER 6

HE ARRIVED at my place at nine fifteen on Saturday. I wasn't expecting him so early. I hadn't shaved and was only wearing boxers. He raised an eyebrow at me.

"Late night?" he asked jokingly.

"No, not at all. I'm just a bum, and you're early. Come on in."

"I didn't interrupt anything, did I?" he asked, glancing toward the bedroom.

I laughed. "God, I wish. The only option for me in this town is Mr. Stevens, the high school band teacher. And he's thirty years older than me. I've never been quite that desperate."

"Glad to hear that." He was headed for the kitchen. "Got any coffee or anything?"

"Sure. Help yourself. Just give me a minute to get dressed."

From the bedroom, I heard the refrigerator open, and then he called out, "Good Lord, don't you have any food?"

"There's food in there!"

"I see milk, beer, a brick of cheese, two carry-out containers, and three—no, make that four!—jars of mustard."

"There you go—milk, beer, and cheese: the three basic food

groups," I told him as I came into the kitchen. "I didn't say there was a lot of food. I don't exactly cook."

"Me neither. Although, I dare say my fridge looks a little better than this." He closed it and turned to me, rubbing his hands in anticipation. "Let's stop by the deli and get some sandwiches to take with us. I'm starving already."

I wasn't sure our sandwich shop (I couldn't quite call it a deli) would be open yet, but we could at least hit the grocery store.

"You ready?" he asked.

"All set."

"Great. We'll get some food, then, um"—why was he looking so flustered?—"we need to stop by and pick up Cherie on our way out of town."

I felt like he had just punched me in the stomach. "Cherie?"

He at least had the decency to look miserable. "I know. Here's the deal: A few nights ago, we got a call for a domestic disturbance. And it turned out to be her house. Her loser ex-husband—what's his name again?"

"Dan Snyder."

"Right. He was there. He was so drunk he could hardly stand up. She was crying, and he was screaming, calling her a whore and worse. And it looked like maybe he had hit her, too, but of course she denied it. On domestic calls, we have to take somebody in, so we arrested him. And that got ugly.

"Anyway, she tracked me down the next day. She showed up at my house, for Christ's sake. Said she wanted to *thank* me, so would I come to dinner at her place? She didn't seem to want to take no for an answer. So I got her to agree to come along with us today instead. Seemed a lot safer than going alone to her house." He sighed and then cocked his eyebrow at me, one corner of his mouth barely twitching up. I was beginning to realize this was what amounted to a smile for him. "Consider yourself our chaperone."

"So you need me to defend your virtue?" I was trying not to smile.

"Not my virtue so much as my independence."

"I'm defending your independence?"

He winked at me. "Exactly."

I had to laugh. "Sweet! I've always wanted to be a goddamn freedom fighter. But you're definitely going to owe me a beer for this one!"

He looked enormously relieved. "I promise."

Knowing that he wasn't too interested in seeing her made me feel a little better. It was obvious when we picked her up that Matt hadn't really clarified that they weren't going to be alone. She wasn't any happier to see me than I was to see her. Still, she seemed determined to make the best of it. I got out of the Jeep and started to climb into the back.

"Jared, don't be silly. With your long legs, you'll be miserable back there. It's no problem for me to sit in the back." I guess chivalry really is dead, because I didn't argue. She obviously did not consider me a rival for his attention. And why would she? I had to remind myself that I wasn't. She situated herself in the middle of the back seat so she could easily lean forward between the seats to talk to us, and we set off.

We had the GPS location of the cache. Given that and a hand-held GPS, it seemed like it should be easy to find the spot. But actually, finding a way there turned out to be surprisingly difficult. We had a big book of topographical maps, which would have been great if they hadn't been ten years old. We spent several hours roaming the high country, trying to find the trail that would take us to the little box of goodies.

"So, Matt, where did you move here from?" Cherie asked.

"I've lived a lot of places. Oklahoma most recently, but I've also lived in Texas, Arkansas, and Kansas City." He looked pointedly at me when he said that last one.

I laughed at him. "That explains it! I was wondering why a boy from Oklahoma would be a Kansas City Chiefs fan! Now that you're here in Colorado, where we have a *real* team, you really need to change your tune. I'll take you to a game, and you can be converted by the Mile High Magic!"

"You Coloradoans are so deluded. You think Mile High is so great? You ever been to Arrowhead? Those people know how to tailgate! Barbecue cooking all day all over the lot. You can smell it for miles. You Broncos fans have a lot to learn!"

"I love barbecue as much as the next man, but it really doesn't justify cheering for a mediocre team, does it?" I was still laughing, and although his expression was still pretty guarded, I could tell he was having fun.

"Mediocre? We only finished one game behind you last season, and that's only because our running back was out for half the season. I bet—"

"So ," Cherie cut in from the back seat. We both jumped a little, and I realized I wasn't the only one who had forgotten she was there. "You have temporary plates. Is this Jeep new?"

"Yeah, I bought it from Jared."

"Oh really? Jared, I didn't think you owned a car."

I was glad she couldn't see me roll my eyes. "I *own* a car. I just prefer riding my bike." Why did everybody think that was so weird? "Anyway, technically he bought it from Lizzy."

"It's great for the trails here, isn't it?"

"That's partly why I bought it. Speaking of trails, some of the guys at the station were talking about Culver's Trail?"

31

"Never heard of it," Cherie said.

But he was looking at me. "Culver's Trail isn't a four-wheel drive trail," I told him. "It's for hiking and biking. It's one of the easier mountain biking trails around."

"Really? They said it was pretty tough."

I grinned at him. "They must be wimps. Hey! Are you planning on buying a mountain bike?" Suddenly the idea of having somebody to ride with had me excited.

"Should I?"

"Absolutely!"

We finally found the spot. We dug up the metal box and opened it up. In addition to the log book, it had an assortment of random items inside: a green plastic army man, a playing card, a ten sided die. We hadn't thought to bring anything with us to add, so we settled for writing our names in the log book and then headed back to the Jeep.

"Shotgun!" Cherie called. She looked a little embarrassed about having said it, but I understood.

"That's only fair, since you had the back seat on the way up." But it didn't work. Matt was still talking to me more than to her. Back in town, she gave it one more try. "Are you sure you don't want to come in for a drink?"

"Thanks, Cherie, but Jared's sister-in-law is expecting us at her house for dinner." I was surprised at the lie but tried to nod convincingly. "Have a great night."

He seemed to be happy that she was gone.

"Great!" he said happily. "Let's go get that beer I owe you!"

"Matt, you do realize that this is a pretty small town. Anywhere we go, there's a chance she'll see us and know you lied."

"Oh." All the wind had gone out of his sails now. "I hadn't

thought of that."

The idea of spending another hour or two together definitely sounded better than going back to my empty house, and I was pleasantly surprised that he seemed to feel the same way. "We actually could go to Lizzy's. It's Saturday. She's probably halfway expecting me to show up."

Brian wasn't home, but Lizzy was. And, as I had predicted, she wasn't surprised to see me. She did, however, raise her eyebrows at Matt. He excused himself to find the bathroom, and she immediately turned on me.

"On a date?" She narrowed her blue eyes at me.

"It's not a date!"

"It looks like a date."

"It's not."

"He sure seems to be spending a lot of time with you."

"He's new in town. He doesn't know anybody. That's all."

"Jarhead," she said in exasperation, "if you think that man doesn't have other options, even in this town, then you must be blind. He chose you."

I knew she was right. Hadn't I just seen him lie to Cherie so that he could spend the evening with me? And she wasn't the only single woman in town by any means. She might have been the only one who had gone to the trouble to track him down at his house, but that only meant she was the most aggressive of the lot. But he was adamant about being straight, so where did that leave us? I could feel myself blushing as I thought about it.

"What are you two talking about?" Matt asked as he strode back into the room. "Looks like you're embarrassing Jared."

"Hair," Lizzy said, without missing a beat. "Can you believe that mess he has on his head? I keep telling him to get it cut!"

33

Matt frowned at me and inspected the dirty mop on my head. I tried not to flinch under his scrutiny. I suddenly had great pity for the monkeys at the zoo.

Then he turned to Lizzy, eyebrow up, a ghost of a grin on his face, and said, "I like it." And that's when I knew I was a complete fool, because my heart swelled up and threatened to burst through my chest, and I knew I was turning tomato red. Matt had already turned and vanished into the kitchen.

"I don't know who he thinks he's fooling," Lizzy hissed at me across the room, "but this is definitely a date!"

CHAPTER 7

HE DROPPED by the shop several times after that, always right at closing time, and we went out for dinner. I was surprised that he seemed to be seeking me out, but I was thrilled at the same time. He was easy to talk to.

Lizzy invited him to her house for a Memorial Day barbecue. He seemed happy to be included, but two days before it was supposed to take place he came into the shop to cancel.

"Lizzy, you're going to have to give me a rain check on dinner. My parents decided to drop in for a visit this week."

"No problem," she said, without even looking up from her inventory list. "Bring them along!"

He looked a little startled by that but said firmly, "No, I couldn't do that."

Now she looked up. "Why not?"

"I couldn't intrude like that."

"Don't be silly. The more the merrier!"

"Ummm." He suddenly looked terribly uncomfortable. "I appreciate that Lizzy, but it's really a bad idea. You'll end up regretting it. Trust me."

"My goodness, are they that bad?" she said jokingly, raising her eyebrows at him.

But he didn't seem to be joking at all when he answered her. "Yeah. They really are. You know that nasty uncle in all the movies who ruins every holiday? That's my dad. No kidding."

She looked at him for a minute, tapping her finger on her lip, like she was trying to decide how serious he was. And then she got that determined look on her face, and I wanted to tell him he might as well give up now, because Lizzy would get what she wanted. "Matt, you've never met my parents. They're insane. I'm talking certifiable wack-a-doo. Jared?" She turned to me. "Tell Matt. My parents are totally fucking loony."

"Well—"

She was already talking to Matt again. "Seriously. Your parents can't possibly be any worse than mine."

"I don't know—"

"Great! Then we'll see you at five thirty!" She looked back down at her inventory list as if the topic was closed.

Matt looked a little baffled, like he wasn't quite sure what had just happened. "Oh. Okay. Well, thanks, Lizzy." He cocked his eyebrow at her, although she was still looking down, so only I saw it. "Don't say I didn't warn you." He turned and walked to the door but then turned at the last minute. "Lizzy, my dad drinks a lot." It sounded like a warning.

"No problem."

THEY arrived right on time. Matt's mom, Lucy, was about five-four, big boned but skinny, with hair that was somewhere in the transition from brown to gray. Her green eyes looked sad and

36

nervous, and her fingers never held still. She fidgeted with her necklace, her earrings, and her hair constantly.

His dad, Joseph, was big. He was as tall as Matt with the same dark hair and military cut. He had obviously once had the same athletic physique as well, but now had a tiny bit of a beer belly and the red, bulbous nose of a hardcore drinker.

They brought a bottle of wine with them, all wrapped up in a pretty foil bag with a bow. As soon as Lucy handed it to Lizzy, Joseph said, "I'll take a glass of that now, if you would."

Matt and I followed Lizzy into the kitchen. Matt was definitely not himself. I had never seen him act so nervous and unsure of himself. His parents were obviously a bomb, and he was just waiting for them to go off.

"We'll definitely have enough to drink," Lizzy said cheerfully, as she opened the wine. "I bought three bottles of wine, two red, one white, and a case of beer. And there's plenty of hard stuff in the cabinet, too, if he wants something stronger." She pointed to the liquor cabinet, before taking the open wine and several glasses, and headed back into the living room.

I started to follow her, but suddenly Matt grabbed my arm. When I looked up, I was surprised to see something like terror on his face. "Why did she buy all that alcohol?"

"You said your dad likes to drink."

"Oh no," he groaned, and covered his face with his hands.

"What's wrong?"

"I meant that she *shouldn't* have alcohol. It was supposed to be a warning. Oh my God, I'm such an idiot. I should have been more clear. Shit! This is bad, Jared. He's a jerk when he's sober. He's an angry, belligerent, antagonistic asshole when he's not."

"That bad?" I would have laughed if he hadn't looked so terrified.

"Yes!" He rubbed his hands hard over his face and then went over to the liquor cabinet and rummaged around, emerging with a bottle of Jack Daniels. He took two glasses out of the cabinet and poured two extra large shots. "Here." He handed one to me and downed his in one swallow.

"I hate this stuff."

"Trust me," he said as he poured another one for himself. "It won't be quite so painful if you're half drunk too."

He was wrong. It was still painful.

We had dinner on the patio. The sun was still up but low in the sky, casting long shadows across the lawn. It was a beautiful night, contrasting strangely with the tension at the table as we stumbled through small talk. Of course, with my family, the conversation eventually turned to football.

"Are you a Chiefs fan too?" Brian asked Joseph.

"Hell, no. I'm a Cowboys fan. I think Matt picked another team just to be rebellious. At least he didn't pick the damn Redskins."

"I was pretty sure you would have thrown me out of the house for that one," Matt said dryly.

"Damn right." I couldn't tell if he was joking or not.

"Lucy," Mom jumped in, "do you work outside of the home?"

Lucy looked a little startled, as if she hadn't realized she might have to speak during dinner. "No, not anymore. I was a nurse for twenty-five years, but I'm retired now."

"Did you work at a hospital or in an office?"

"In a hospital. I worked in several departments over the years, but what I loved the most was the maternity ward. I was there for the last ten years. All those babies." For the first time her hands were still, held together in front of her like she praying. She smiled nostalgically and turned to Lizzy. "When are you due?"

"Halloween."

Lucy turned to Mom. She was still smiling but looking sad at the same time. "I envy you. I keep hoping for a grandchild." She glanced at Matt and then back at the table in front of her. Suddenly her smile was gone and she was fidgeting again. She looked like she regretted having said that. I realized why when Joseph opened his mouth.

"Doesn't look to me like you're ever going to get one so you might as well quit hoping. As far as I can tell, Matt isn't ever going to do his duty in that department."

"You might have noticed that I'm not physically capable of producing a child on my own." There was not a hint of humor in his voice. Matt was staring at his plate. I had a feeling this was not a new argument.

"Don't be a smartass with me. It's past time for you to marry and settle down. You're not getting any younger."

"We're planning a vacation," Lucy said suddenly, in a desperately obvious ploy to change the subject.

Lizzy jumped in with her. "That's great, Lucy. Where are you going?"

"Florida, I think, although I don't know if we should go to—"

"Are you dating anyone?" Joseph did not seem to be aware that the topic of conversation had been changed.

"No, Dad. I've been busy. It's not that easy to meet people."

I was actually a little surprised at that, since I knew there were several single women in town who would have killed for a date with him.

"Bullshit! What about Jared here?" I just about jumped out of my chair. For half a second, I thought he was suggesting that Matt

39

date *me*. But then he went on. "I'm sure he can introduce you to someone. Jared, you have a girlfriend, right?"

"Uh," I was feeling terribly off balance, considering what a simple question it was. "No, sir."

"Why the hell not?"

"Well." Matt was turning toward me with sheer horror in his eyes, trying to warn me, but it was too late. The words were already out of my mouth. "I'm gay."

Matt's head went down, elbows on the table and fingers laced behind his head like somebody had just yelled "duck and cover." Lucy's mouth formed an O of surprise, and her fidgety fingers went in to overdrive.

"You're gay?" Joseph's voice was terribly loud and slightly slurred. "You mean you're a fag?"

"Well...." I was looking around the table for help, but there didn't seem to be any forthcoming. They were all frozen in states of dreadful anticipation. Our dinner had turned into some kind of movie of the week, and no matter how poorly acted it was, nobody seemed to be changing the channel.

"So you like to fuck other men up the ass?"

That woke them all up. Everybody at the table jumped a little when he said that, but Lizzy recovered quickest. She turned back to Lucy and said loudly, "I'm sorry, Lucy. I missed what you said. Where in Florida are you going?"

Lucy was visibly shaking now, fidgeting with her necklace. "Well, I was thinking of Fort Lauderdale, but I'm not sure if only kids go there. Maybe Orlando? Have you been there?"

"I haven't, but my brother—"

Lizzy didn't get to tell us any more about her brother.

Joseph suddenly stood up, knocking his chair over behind him in the process. Matt looked up, startled, as Joseph pointed a finger at me and said, "Are you fucking my son? Is that what's going on here?"

"No!" Matt and I both said in unison, and Matt said, "Dad, enough!"

"Joseph!" Lucy's voice was a quiet plea. "We are guests here. Sit down."

He didn't listen. "I knew a man like you in the Marines," he said to me. "Married and everything, and one day his wife comes home and finds him fucking another man in her bed. Earned himself a dishonorable discharge."

Matt's hands were white knuckled fists on the table in front of him. "You were friends with James for six years before that happened, Dad. Remember that? He was a good guy."

"You don't know what you're talking about."

"He was your friend. You should have stood by him."

"You don't know what it's like in the Marines. You took the sucker's way out. Don't try to talk to me about what I should or shouldn't have done. You don't know a goddamn thing about it." He picked up his wine glass and frowned at it blurrily when he saw that it was empty. He picked up Lucy's and drained it. Then he grabbed the open bottle off of the table and went back into the house, leaving the rest of us in uncomfortable silence on the patio.

After a minute, Lucy stood up too. Her hands were shaking, and I could tell she was close to tears. "Matt, I think you should take us back to the motel now. We've intruded on your friends enough for one evening." She straightened her shirt and her skirt, smoothed her hair, and put herself back together before turning to Lizzy. "It was very nice meeting you all. Thank you for a lovely dinner." I think she would have said more, but her chin had started to quiver, and she quickly retreated to the house.

41

Nobody else moved. Brian looked stunned. Mom looked pissed. Lizzy looked like she was replaying the whole dinner in her mind, trying to figure out where things went wrong. Matt was just sitting there, staring at his plate. Finally he raised his eyes to Lizzy. "Lizzy, I'm sorry."

She looked over at him and gave him a sad smile. She held her hand out to him, palm up on the table. He obligingly put his large hand over hers. She put her other hand on top and patted it. "You warned me. Next time you tell me something is a bad idea, I'll listen."

He relaxed a little at that and nodded. "Thanks, Lizzy." He turned to me, opened his mouth to say something, then glanced at everybody else still sitting around the table, and seemed to change his mind. Instead, he just clapped me on the back and said, "I'll see you later."

After he left, we all sat there in silence. I felt miserable. If I hadn't been such an idiot, none of it would have happened. Why did I have to open my big mouth? "Lizzy, I'm so sorry. I shouldn't have—"

"No!" Her eyes were fierce. "Don't apologize! Don't you dare apologize for that bigoted asshole." She got up, came around the table and hugged my shoulders from behind my chair. "He's a jerk, and you have nothing to be sorry about."

CHAPTER 8

"JARED!" Ringo crashed through the door of the shop at top speed, knocking over a display of car air fresheners. He didn't stop but ran back to where I stood at the back. "Jared, I passed! I got a ninety-seven on the test!" He flew at me and threw his skinny arms around my neck.

"That's great!" I patted him awkwardly on the back, and he seemed to realize what he was doing and stepped back. His face was glowing triumphantly, and he was grinning ear to ear.

"You're a genius!" he told me.

I couldn't help catching a little of his good mood. "You did the work, not me. Come on! I'll take you out for a beer to celebrate."

"I'm not twenty-one."

"I didn't say the beer would be for you! Let's go."

I took him to our local pizza joint, Tony's. We ordered our pizza, and the waitress had just dropped off my beer and a root beer for Ringo when Matt appeared at our table.

"Hey Jared!" He looked genuinely pleased to see me but a little wary. "How have you been?"

"Great. Ringo here just aced his algebra final, and we're celebrating." Ringo still hadn't stopped smiling.

43

"That's great," Matt told him but then turned back to me. "Mind if I sit down for a minute?"

"Of course I don't mind."

He slid into the booth next to me. "Jared, I owe you an apology for what happened at dinner—"

"Don't worry about it."

"My dad—"

"I don't really care what your dad thinks of me, Matt. You were right. He's an angry, belligerent, antagonistic asshole."

"Eventually you'll learn that I'm usually right." His eyes crinkled, like he was almost laughing, so I knew that was a joke. "No hard feelings then?"

"None at all."

"Thanks, Jared." He sounded enormously relieved and clapped me on the back hard enough to knock the wind out of me. "You know, we've got a table over there. Why don't you boys come and join us?"

I looked in the direction he was pointing. Two cops and three women. In other words, complete hell. One look at Ringo's face told me he wasn't any more excited about the idea than I was.

"I don't think that's a good idea."

"Sure it is! Come on! Save me, please. I'm not sure how I got sucked into this dinner. I thought I was having drinks with the guys, and now I find out I'm on a blind date."

"Jesus!" I laughed at him. "Then I'm *really* not going over there!"

"Can I stay here then?" He gave me the look I was starting to think of as the pseudo-smile: one eyebrow cocked, the corner of his mouth twitching up.

"You're joking, right?"

44

He rubbed a hand over his close-cropped dark hair and said tiredly, "Only partially."

"Is she that bad?" I looked over at the table. One of the women was definitely keeping her eye on him. She was decent looking, with red hair that was obviously dyed.

"I'm sure she's very nice," he said quietly, "but we have absolutely nothing to say to one another. I've just sat through the most awkward forty minutes of small talk ever. I'll have more fun if you're there. Just come over, and we can talk football until they get bored and leave."

"Matt, there's no way those guys are going to accept me sitting with them."

"Sure they will." But he didn't sound sure.

"They won't. Are you going to tell me that they haven't already given you a hard time for hanging out with me?"

I could tell by the flush in his cheeks that I was right, but he didn't give up. "That's part of the point, Jared. Maybe if you spent some time with them, they would realize—"

"Trust me. It's a bad idea. Anyway, I owe Ringo here a celebration pizza."

He glanced over at Ringo in surprise, as if he had forgotten he was there, but then conceded with a dramatic sigh. "Fine. Send me to my doom. They won't leave me alone until I'm engaged. I'll send you an invitation to the wedding."

"I would offer to host your bachelor party, but I don't think you'd like my choice of strippers."

He actually laughed at that. I had never heard him laugh before, and I foolishly found myself thinking that it was the most wondrous sound in the world. "See? I told you. You're more fun."

CHAPTER 9

A WEEK later, Matt showed up on my doorstep just after five o'clock. He still had his uniform on. I was glad to see him.

"Let's go," he said as soon as I opened the door. "I'll buy you dinner."

Once we were in the Jeep, he said, "I need to stop by my place on the way. I want to change." I hadn't been to his house yet and was curious to see how he lived.

It turned out that he didn't live in a house at all. He pulled up in front of a strip of apartments. Had it been bigger, it might have been called a condo. It was a long narrow rectangle of white brick, containing four claustrophobic one-bedroom flats.

We walked in the door, and I was stunned by the sterile emptiness of the place. Most of the tiny living room was taken up by one of those giant strength-building home gyms you see on TV. In addition to that, there was one metal folding chair, an old wooden end table (being used as a coffee table, in front of the one chair), and a TV sitting on a milk crate. And it was the cleanest bachelor pad I had ever seen.

"Wow. Nice place. The prison cell motif is really working for you. Very feng shui."

He gave me the pseudo-smile: cocked eyebrow and one side of

his mouth twitching up. "Here I've been thinking you weren't really gay, and then you go and use words like 'motif' and 'feng shui.'" I had to laugh at that. "Make yourself at home," he called over his shoulder as he went into the bedroom to change.

The cliché sentiment sounded ridiculous; nothing had ever felt less like a home.

Behind the living room, next to what passed for a kitchen, was a nook that couldn't quite be called a dining room. It held a rickety card table and another metal folding chair. But I was surprised to see that the entire back wall was taken up by a large book case stuffed full to bursting. I walked over to browse the titles. They were crammed in every which way, but I soon realized that they were sorted by genre and were roughly alphabetical by author. Talk about neat and tidy. One shelf was law-related, police procedurals, and criminal justice textbooks. Then more non-fiction, mostly related to war and the military, but also a few biographies and a huge assortment of fiction—mystery, horror, sci-fi, Westerns, and even a few graphic novels.

Matt emerged from the bedroom, dressed in his usual jeans and T-shirt. He stood beside me, tall and straight with his hands behind his back, looking at those books. I felt like I had found a tiny window into his heart. Or a shrine, but I didn't know to what.

"You never struck me as much of a reader."

He was silent for a moment and then said quietly, "I'm alone a lot. Sometimes it's hard to fill the hours."

Those words and the hint of tired resignation in his voice, struck a chord inside me—they echoed my own loneliness so completely. "I know exactly what you mean."

And in that moment, something passed between us. We didn't speak, but I knew we both felt it. It wasn't anything as trite or romantic as finding one's soul mate. It was simply a silent recognition that we truly were kindred spirits. That we had both been alone for a long time and maybe we didn't need to be anymore.

"SO YOUR family doesn't mind that you're gay." It was more a statement than a question.

We were at Tony's. Matt refused to go to Mamacita's, where he risked running into Cherie. It wasn't really much better here. I was sure we were the only table that had two waitresses rushing to serve us. He didn't seem to notice.

"It bothered my dad a little. He thought, like you did, that I just hadn't tried hard enough. He would actually say things like, 'You just need to take one or two out for a test drive, son.' My mom took it pretty well. But sometimes it makes her sad, because she knows I'll be missing out on having kids. And she hates seeing me alone. Brian does his best to be cool with it, although it still freaks him out a bit, I think. Back when I came out, he was the one I was most worried about. I always looked up to him, and I was sure he would hate me. I decided that he had to be the first person I told, and it took me forever to get up the nerve. So, I took him out to a bar—I had just turned twenty-one—and had a couple of drinks to get up my courage, and I finally said, 'Brian, I'm gay.' And, he laughed. He actually laughed, and said, 'No kidding, kid? Did you finally figure it out?'" I laughed again, thinking back on it. Of course Brian, who always kept his eye on me, had figured it out sometime between my Steve Atwater outburst and my infatuation with his best friend and my twenty-first birthday. "It was all rather anticlimactic, but it was also a relief to know that I hadn't changed in his estimation. I couldn't have handled that."

"Do you have a, you know, a—um—*friend*?"

He seemed to stumble on that word, and I laughed at him. "I have one *friend*, sort of. His name is Cole. We met in college. He was dating my roommate, actually. But after they broke up, he and I

48

hooked up a couple of times. He lives in Arizona, but his family owns a condo in Vail, and sometimes when he's up here skiing, he'll call and we'll get together. It's very casual. We're not really each other's type. He's too flamboyant for me, and I'm too small town for him. It is occasionally mutually convenient and with absolutely zero strings attached. But other than that, no. There's no one."

"But how do you meet people? I mean, others like you?"

"I don't. Not anymore. I used to go to the clubs sometimes. There's one in Fort Collins and a couple in Boulder and a bunch in Denver. But, you know, it's just like it is for straight guys. You might be able to get laid—well, at a gay club, it's almost a guarantee that you *can* get laid, depending on your standards—but you're never gonna find anything more than that."

"Is that what you want? Something more?"

"Don't we all?" That came out sounding way too pretentious. We definitely needed to change the subject. "So how's work?" I could tell right away that was a bad question. His grey eyes darkened—I couldn't see the green at all right now—and he tensed up a little.

"Not great," he said darkly.

"What's up? Is there a crime wave in Coda I haven't heard about?"

He loosened up a little. "I've had to drag Dan Snyder away from Cherie's house two more times. The first time, he was drunk and throwing bottles at her house. The other time, he was inside, and she looked bad. I don't get it. She won't press charges, but it was pretty obvious he had been beating on her again. He's a real piece of work."

"Dan was always a fuckup. Even in high school."

"Yeah." He was quiet for a minute and then started pulling at the label on his beer bottle. "I'm getting a lot of shit from the other

49

guys," he said quietly. He didn't look at me, and it took a second for me to figure it out.

"Because of me?"

A reluctant nod.

"Then what the hell are we doing here?" I asked incredulously. I had to tell myself to keep my voice down. "You come to my house and bring me out to dinner—of course they're going to talk."

He just shrugged. "It pisses me off." He didn't sound pissed though; he sounded sad. "They don't know what it's like. They're all married. The other night when I saw you here—that's not the first time. They're always trying to set me up." I wasn't sure what to say to that. "I work with them, so I want to get along with them, but at the end of the day, they go home to their families." And he went home alone to his prison cell of an apartment. He didn't say that part, but I heard it.

We ate in silence for a bit, and then a voice said, "Hello, Jared!" I looked up to see Mr. Stevens, the high school band director and the only other gay man in town, as far as I knew. He was in his sixties and well dressed. He seemed to always have on a bow tie.

"Hey, Mr. Stevens. How's life?"

"You haven't been my student for a long time. You know you can call me Bill." He always told me this, but it's hard to call any former teacher by their first name. "And I believe you are our newest police officer?" he said to Matt.

"Yes, sir. Matt Richards." He shook Mr. Steven's slightly limp hand.

"Mr. Richards, it is very nice to meet you. I'm so glad you've joined our tiny community. I hope you don't mind me asking, but are you actually out with the department?"

I was trying not to smile. It was obvious that Mr. Stevens assumed Matt was gay. But it was equally obvious, to me, at least, that Matt had no idea what Mr. Stevens meant. I could tell by the look on his face that he was thinking, "out where?" But he nodded gamely and said, "Yes, sir, I am." Now I was really having a hard time not laughing.

"That's fabulous! I'm glad to hear that our department is so progressive." Matt's demeanor barely changed. Mr. Stevens obviously could not tell how confused he was, and I realized that I was becoming quite adept at reading his guarded expressions. "Well, I'll leave you two alone. I want you to know that it makes me so happy to see you two together." He winked at me. "It gives an old man hope."

"Thanks, Mr. Stevens. You know I wish you luck."

When he was gone, Matt looked at me and said, "What the hell? What was that guy talking about? And what's so damn funny?"

"Don't you remember me telling you about Mr. Stevens, the band director?"

I watched him as he thought about it and saw the light come on. Then his eyes shifted from side to side as he replayed the conversation in his head, and a blush crept up his cheeks as the pieces fell into place.

"Finally figured it out, did you?"

"Shit." He didn't seem mad so much as annoyed at himself. "Sometimes I'm such an idiot."

"Well, I wouldn't worry about it. Mr. Stevens knows all about discretion."

"I guess that's probably true."

"Does it bother you that he thinks we're together?"

"Does it bother you?"

"Not at all."

"You and he never...?" I noticed he had evaded my question

51

but let it pass.

"Never. I don't think either one of us has ever even considered it. There's a pretty big age difference, obviously. And he was my teacher once, so that would be pretty fucking weird. And I don't know for sure, but I suspect Mr. Stevens likes his men a little more feminine, if you know what I mean."

"And how do you like your men?" His cheeks were bright red, but his gaze was level on mine.

And boy did that feel like the trick question of the month. Because of course, I liked my men just like him: tall and dark and muscular. The only thing I might have added was longer hair and tattoos—and I had to wonder if there were any under his shirt. But I couldn't say it.

What I said was, "Filthy rich."

He gave me the pseudo-smile. I had a feeling that he knew the real answer.

CHAPTER 10

HE BEGAN to stop by the shop at closing time again, and we had dinner together two or three times a week. Every time, I asked him if it was causing trouble for him at work. At first he would just shrug, but by the third week, the question was making him blush. That confused me.

"I don't understand. Does it cause problems for you or not?"

"Well, it did," he said hesitantly. "But I've made some changes over the past few weeks that have helped." He wasn't looking at me when he said it.

"'Changes'? Like what?"

"I actually, umm…." He was fidgeting with the label on his beer bottle again. "I started seeing Cherie."

"What?"

He glanced up at me and gave me the pseudo-smile. "You heard me."

"You're dating Cherie?"

"No. *Not* dating."

"But you just said—"

"What I said was I started *seeing* her. Not the same thing." He

53

said it like it was the most obvious thing in the world. I was still confused, and my face must have shown it, because he rolled his eyes at me and said, "Let's just say we have an arrangement. Like you and your friend, Cole."

"Ahh. I see." Now I was having a hard time keeping a straight face. "Occasionally mutually convenient?"

He shrugged. "Well, convenient for me, at any rate."

"I thought you valued your independence?"

"I do. But I'm not exactly a fan of celibacy either."

"Who is?"

He winked at me. "Exactly."

"Why her? I mean, not to be a jerk, but she's got, well...."

"A reputation?" He was back to picking at the label on the bottle.

"Right." I was relieved that it wasn't news to him.

He shrugged. "I wear a raincoat."

That actually made me blush. "Well, that's good, but that's not what I meant."

"She seemed like the best bet for a 'no strings' type of relationship. I have absolutely no interest in anything more serious."

"And she's actually in agreement with that?" I certainly couldn't claim to be an expert on women, but I had always suspected that "no strings attached" was a lot harder for them than for men.

"Look"—and I could tell he was getting a little annoyed that he had to explain it to me—"I'm not a total asshole. I have been completely honest with her. She knows that we're not dating. There will be no romantic moonlight strolls or anniversary dinners. I'm not meeting her parents, or buying her flowers, or moving in with her, or even meeting her friends. We fuck. That's it."

"She's actually okay with that?"

"She says that she is." He shrugged again. "I'm sure she thinks that I will change my mind over time. I won't, and I've told her that I won't. It's not my fault if she chooses not to believe me." I couldn't help but think that Cherie might be right. I figured after a few weeks, he wouldn't object so much to "dating." I was pretty sure the way to a man's heart was actually a little lower than the stomach. "She has requested only that I be 'faithful,' and not date or sleep with any other women while we're seeing one another."

"And that's acceptable to you?"

"Absolutely. The whole point is to keep the complications to a bare minimum, and adding another woman to the mix would definitely qualify as a 'complication'."

"Yes, I suppose it would."

"Plus, the arrangement has other benefits." He had the pseudo-smile again.

"Such as?"

He actually almost smiled over at me now. "First, the guys at work are no longer trying to set me up. And, more importantly, I am now free to hang out with you as much as I like without having to put up with annoying accusations."

"So let me get this straight: you're willing to have sex, no strings attached, with a hot bimbo, just so you can hang out with me more?"

His green-in-grey eyes were sparkling, crinkling at the corners like he was about to laugh. "It is quite a sacrifice on my part, I admit. Don't say I never did anything for you."

"Wow." I couldn't help but laugh. "You are a manipulative bastard."

"I am. I can't deny that." He said it lightly but then suddenly became serious. "Are you thoroughly disgusted?"

"By the idea of you fucking Cherie? A little. By the fact that you're a manipulative bastard? Not so much. She's a big girl, and if you really are being honest with her—"

"I am."

"Then it's just a matter of consenting adults."

"Exactly." He seemed relieved to have that out of the way. "So, what about your friend Cole? How often do you get to see him?"

"He's only here during prime ski season, but I usually see him two or three times between December and the first of April."

"So never between April and December?"

"Right."

"Wow," he said sympathetically, "that's a hell of a dry season."

"Tell me about it."

Our food came then and put an end to that depressing topic.

"Are you working next weekend?" he asked as I started to eat.

"Yeah."

"Can you get it off?"

Getting the weekend off would actually be easy. Since it was summer vacation, Ringo was able to work full-time. Plus, Lizzy was willing to take more hours than usual, because we both knew that once the baby came in the fall, the tables would be turned.

"Sure. What's up?"

"I'll be working overtime on July third and fourth, but then I have a three-day weekend after that, starting Friday. I thought we could go camping. I bought a bike last week, too, so we could do some riding."

I was elated. I always loved spending time in the mountains, but usually I had to go alone. Sometimes Brian and Lizzy would go with me, but between Brian's job and the shop, it was hard for us all to get away together. The idea of having company, especially *Matt's* company, was exhilarating. "That sounds great!"

"Should I pick you up?"

"Yeah. Come by early on Friday. We can get breakfast first, then get our gear together, and head up."

"I'll be there."

"Are you planning on inviting Cherie?"

He looked up at me, horrified. "Why would I want to ruin a perfectly good weekend?"

CHAPTER 11

HE WAS knocking on my door at seven thirty on Friday morning. I was still in bed.

"Jesus Christ," I groaned as I let him in. "When I said early, I didn't mean at the butt crack of fucking dawn." I'm not good at being cheery before nine o'clock.

He didn't quite laugh but was obviously amused. His eyes crinkled at the sides a bit, and he smacked me playfully on the back of the head. "What are you talking about? The sun's been up for almost two hours now."

"Oh man, I hate morning people." I went into the kitchen and started making coffee. "For the record, 'early' means 'before lunch.'"

That actually made him laugh. I had now heard him laugh exactly two times. And yes, I was counting.

We went out for breakfast first and then started getting our gear together.

"Make sure you pack plenty of warm clothes," I told him.

"What do I need warm clothes for? It's summer!"

"We're gonna be camping at over ten thousand feet. It'll be

cold when the sun goes down, believe me!"

"Where exactly is the campground?" Matt asked suspiciously.

"The *what*?" I was laughing.

"We're not going to a campground?" His confused look made me laugh even harder.

"Hell, no! We're going somewhere better than any campground!"

We were loaded up and on our way out of town by eleven o'clock.

He followed my directions, farther up into the national forest, then onto a dirt road, and from there, onto a rocky four-wheel drive track.

He glanced around us doubtfully. We were headed crossways up the side of the mountain. The ground rose sharply up on our left and dropped just as quickly on the right. "Are you sure you know where you're going?"

I grinned over at him. "Trust me."

I showed him where to pull off the side of the road—there was just enough room in this spot to get the Jeep off the trail—and we started unloading. He was still looking around skeptically.

"We'll probably have to make two trips," I said as I handed him the cooler.

"How far are we walking?"

"Not far. It's sort of steep though, so don't try to carry too much at once. The shitty part is carrying it back up here on Sunday."

He followed me down the hill through bushes and trees. There wasn't much of a path, but I didn't need one. We went down about a hundred yards to where the ground leveled off and then turned right for about another thirty until we reached a small clearing.

59

Not many people knew about our spot. My family had been coming here since I was a kid, and the location was a secret we guarded jealously. We had teased Brian that we knew he was actually going to marry Lizzy when he finally brought her for the first time.

We had a large fire pit with rocks Brian and I had collected piled about a foot high around it. We had benches, made by my father and grandfather from old logs. Some families have second homes. This was ours.

Once there, I dropped my gear and just stood there, soaking it in. Behind us on the right was one of the large rocky abutments like the one Matt and I had climbed the day we met. In front of us was the river. Well, in Colorado, it's a river. In most of the rest of the country, it would probably be called a stream. My grandpa called it a creek (when he said it, it sounded like "crick"). It's about fifteen feet to the opposite bank, only about two or three feet deep but rushing fast over its rocky bed. In places, you could cross on the giant rocks without getting your feet wet as long as you didn't slip on the wet stone. The sun was shining through the trees, and the water splashing off of the rocks created hundreds of tiny prisms over the river. Our side of the stream was mostly evergreens, but directly across from us was a grove of aspens, leaves rustling in the breeze.

I stood and let the feeling of that place fill me. I have often wondered if this was what religious people feel when they pray. It is a feeling of reverence and awe, serenity and belonging. The light breeze, the smell of the forest, the rushing water, the whispering leaves—they seem to fill me, like my soul is opening up and being swept clean. It is the only thing in my life I could call spiritual.

Behind me, I heard Matt say, "Jared, this is amazing."

"It's my favorite place in the world." I knew that sounded childish, but it was true.

"You were right. It's definitely better than any campground."

We set up camp, then spent some time hiking and biking, and cooked hot dogs over the fire for dinner. As the sun went down, we built the fire up higher and started adding layers of warmer clothes. We never seemed to run out of things to talk about. Finally, long after sunset, we let the fire die down to crackling crimson coals and leaned back in our chairs, staring up at the billions of stars that could never be seen in town. The moon was barely a sliver, and the Milky Way was a bright luminescent stripe above us.

Matt's voice in the dark said, "Thanks for bringing me here."

"Thanks for coming."

We finally headed into the tent. We had debated bringing two, but they were all large tents, and in the end, space in the Jeep was limited, so we had agreed to share one.

"This is always the worst part," I said as I stripped down to my boxers. "The trick is to get undressed and into your bag as fast as possible."

"Are you crazy?" he asked. "It's so cold."

"You'll be warmer in your bag without your clothes," I told him as I climbed into my bag. "That way, it's just your body warming the bag, and the bag warming you. The layers of clothes will get in the way. Of course, it's hell when you have to pee in the night. But you'll be warmer. Trust me." I was all zipped up now, starting to feel toasty and already getting drowsy. "You can leave your thermals on if you want." I yawned. "Weren't you a Boy Scout?"

"No. We never stayed anywhere long enough." He was starting to get undressed now. He raised his eyebrow at me playfully and said, "I think this is all just a ploy to get me naked."

I laughed. "You're right. In fact, it's going to be so cold tonight, our only hope for survival is for you to share my bag." He laughed a little at that, too, but then he pulled his shirt off, and it was all I could do not to stare. His body was amazing, just as I had always imagined: strong and lean and heavily muscled. There was no hair on his chest but a little around his navel and a dark trail of it that got thicker as went down to where it disappeared under the waistband of his sweats. I could picture all too clearly the thick, black hair that trail led to. Suddenly the idea of him sharing my bag, although it had been a joke, was foremost in my mind. I couldn't help but imagine having his smooth skin against mine, following that trail with my fingers to the hair below. My body was reacting in a way that would have horrified him, and I was glad that I had managed to get into my bag before he started undressing.

I closed my eyes while he undressed the rest of the way. No need to torment myself any more than I already had. I heard him climb into his bag and zip it up, and then the lantern went off.

It was quiet for a moment, and then he said, "Jared?"

"Hmmm?"

"Good night."

I had embarrassingly erotic dreams about him all night and woke up crazy horny in the morning. He was already up, and I took advantage of the empty tent to try and alleviate my predicament as quickly and quietly as I could. Once I was up and dressed and made it outside, I was happy to find that he had made coffee. He gave me the pseudo-grin as he handed me a cup of it.

"What's so funny?" I asked him.

"You talk in your sleep."

Oh shit! Of course, I knew that I sometimes talked while dreaming, and I tried to sound very casual as I asked, "What did I say?" I was hoping like hell it hadn't been about him.

"You said, 'let me follow it', and I asked 'follow what?', and you said, 'the trail'."

I turned away so he couldn't see me turning red and said, "I was dreaming about mountain biking."

CHAPTER 12

WE SPENT several weeks riding easy trails while he got the hang of mountain riding. He was in good shape, and what he lacked in skill he made up for in endurance. Finally, in early August, we decided to try one of the more challenging trails.

It was a sweltering hot day without even a breeze to cool us off. The stream crossings had all dried to bare trickles. The ground was baked to hard dust. It seemed like nothing was moving in the forest except us.

We were halfway up the trail when I heard him go down behind me. When I turned around, he was lying flat on his back on the dusty trail, but to my amazement, he was smiling. Not the pseudo-smile but a true, genuine, ear-to-ear smile. It was the first time I had seen it, and it was like the sun had finally emerged from behind the clouds.

"Holy shit, that hurt."

"Are you all right?"

"I'll live." He sat up with a groan. "I think I'm getting old." He had a huge scrape down front of his shin. "Hey, look at that!" he said in amazement. "I'm bleeding." I think the smile got bigger.

"It's not a successful ride if you don't bleed."

"Oh really? Did you get that out of the Masochist Biking Club handbook?"

"Sure did. It's rule number three."

I took advantage of the break to try to get my hair back into a ponytail. Curls were escaping all over the place and falling in my face. Matt stood up and inspected the damage to his leg. "The blood's running down into my shoe."

"Rub some dirt on it."

"What?" He was laughing, still wearing that gorgeous smile and looking at me like I was crazy.

"Rub some dirt on it. It'll help stop the bleeding."

"Is that out of the masochist handbook too?"

"I think it's a baseball thing."

"Okay, but if I end up with a raging infection and have to get my leg amputated, I'm holding you responsible."

"I'll pay for your prosthetic."

We made it to the top and stood looking down at the valley below us. He turned to me with that brilliant smile—that made twice I had seen it, and it took my breath away—and said, "The bike was definitely a good idea."

We spent the rest of the summer together. I couldn't remember ever being happier. It was so nice to have a friend to hang out with. At times I couldn't help but wish that it was more, but it was never enough to dampen my enthusiasm for spending time with him. Finally, I wasn't alone. It was the best feeling in the world.

We went camping and mountain biking and geo-caching. We went out to dinner or had dinner with Brian and Lizzy or just sat on my couch drinking beer and watching bad TV. Some nights we even cooked dinner at my house, and then he would help me do the dishes afterward. It felt strangely domestic.

One afternoon I found an old Battleship game in the closet, and we spent several days challenging each other until he caught me cheating. In my family, cheating was always part of the fun, but he was appalled by my blatant disregard for the rules and wouldn't play again after that.

Most of his evenings and days off, he spent with me. I knew he occasionally went to Cherie's house after leaving mine, but true to his word, he did not seem to be interested in pursuing anything else with her. He never mentioned her at all. The couple of times that I half-heartedly suggested he invite her to join us, he looked at me like I had suggested the unthinkable. I didn't mind.

CHAPTER 13

"I BROUGHT stuff to make nachos," Matt said as he came in from the kitchen and handed me a beer.

"You're making nachos?"

He gave me the pseudo-grin. "I thought *you* were making nachos." I threw my bottle cap at him. He ignored it and looked over at the TV. "Pre-season football? What's the point?"

"It's better than no football at all."

"You know," he said teasingly, "I don't think gay guys are supposed to like football."

I rolled my eyes at him. "Yeah, I've heard that before. But so far, nobody's come by to revoke my 'Gay Guys' membership card."

He laughed and then turned back to the TV. "The Cowboys and the Broncos? Damn, I might actually have to cheer for your Broncs on this one."

I laughed in surprise. "Really? I'm amazed."

"I always root against the Cowboys just to piss my dad off."

"I forgot he was a Cowboys fan. I'll have to cheer against them from now on, too, just on general principle."

"Only one more week," he said, and I knew exactly what he

was talking about. We were counting down the days until regular season started. He was the first person I had ever met, not counting my father and Brian, who was as excited about pro football as I was. "And the week after that, we'll be watching my Chiefs kicking ass all over your Broncos," he said. As division rivals, our teams would play each other twice in the season.

"We'll see."

"Loser buys dinner for a week."

"Deal."

He held up his beer, like a toast, but winced a little as he did.

"Are you still sore from that bike crash last week?"

"Yes. Which wouldn't be so bad, except now I can't sleep right. This morning I woke up with a huge knot in my shoulder. I think it's a sign of impending old age."

I said, without really thinking about it, "I can help you with that, you know."

His eyes crinkled at the corners, which meant he was almost laughing. "With old age?"

"No, smartass, with your shoulder."

"How?"

He was sitting forward on the edge of the couch, so it was easy for me to get up and sit on the back of it behind him. "Take off your shirt."

"What?" He twisted around and looked at me in horror like I had just suggested he strip naked and dance for quarters.

"Settle down." I smacked him on the back of the head. "I'm good at this. I used to do it for my mom. She would get knots in her shoulder from painting for hours at a time."

"I'd rather not."

"Look, you don't need to feel weird about it or anything." He looked skeptical. "I'm not making a pass at you, I swear."

"Okay." Maybe a little less skeptical now.

"It hurts, right?"

"Yeah."

"So stop being freaked out and take off your shirt, you baby. This will help. Trust me."

There's nothing as good as calling a big tough guy a baby to get him to do what you want. He thought about it for a second and then shrugged a little. "Okay." He pulled his shirt off and turned back to the TV. "Nothing below the belt." He said it so I knew it was at least halfway a joke, and I laughed.

"I promise."

He was still sitting forward on the couch, not leaning back against me, which made it easier. His back was broad and very muscular. It was certainly nothing like rubbing my mom's small, lax shoulders, and I quickly started to appreciate how strong a person's hands would have to be to do this for a living.

He was tense at first, but as I worked, he started to relax. His head fell forward, and he made a low rumbling sound almost like purring as I worked at the knot, carefully avoiding the huge bruise on the other side from our last bike ride. There was an old scar midway down his back, from his left side to just past his backbone. I had seen it before but never asked him about it. I brushed one finger over it and felt him shudder a little.

"What happened?"

"I was climbing through a barbed wire fence on my grandpa's ranch." He stopped short, and I thought he was done, but a minute later he started talking again. "I was just a kid. It was Easter, and my mom had me dressed up in my nice clothes. I wasn't supposed to go into the pasture, but I wanted to see the horses. I figured she wouldn't ever know, but I kind of tripped going through the fence and got caught on the wire. Ripped a huge hole in my new shirt and got blood all over my pants. I thought for sure my dad was going to tan my ass for that one."

"He didn't?"

"No. My mom sure was mad, but for some reason, my dad just laughed."

"Really?" That was surprising.

"Yeah." He was quiet for a second and then said quietly, "It was a long time ago." And I knew by the way he said it that he didn't want to talk about his dad anymore.

"Brian and I once managed to knock over the entire rack of bulk nails at the shop. Hundreds of loose nails, all different sizes, all over the floor. Maybe thousands, I don't know. A fucking *lot* of nails, I know that much."

"Did you get in trouble?"

"Dad was pissed as hell, but my parents were always big on the idea of punishment fitting the crime."

"So what happened?"

"We spent the next five hours picking them all up and sorting them back into the correct boxes. Customers would come in and see us and start to help, and my dad would say, 'they made that bed of nails themselves, they can clean it up themselves too!'"

Matt laughed a little, and I kept rubbing. His skin was darker than mine and, except for the scar, completely flawless.

"Your grandpa has a ranch?"

"*Had*, past tense. It belonged to my mom's parents, but they're gone now, and the ranch went to my uncle, and he sold it. I had so much fun there as a kid with my cousins. But we didn't go there often. My mom's family never liked my dad much." It seemed we kept coming back to his dad tonight without really meaning to. "For two years, we lived less than thirty miles away from them, and I got to see them almost every weekend. But then we moved again. We never stayed anywhere very long. The longest we stayed in one place was three years, ninth grade through my junior year. And then we moved again two weeks into my senior year. I hated it."

"Is that why you didn't join the military?"

There was a brief hesitation and then, "Part of it." But I knew from his voice that topic wasn't going any further either. "It must have been nice living in the same place your whole life."

"In some ways. But coming back here after college felt a little bit like failure. Like everybody else was moving away, and I was just coming back to my parents. It seemed like only the losers were still stuck here. Like Dan and Cherie." I stopped short, realizing maybe I shouldn't have said that, but he didn't seem to notice, so I went on. "I guess I got used to it. I love it. I love Colorado. I don't think I could ever live away from the mountains. Whenever I get far enough east that I can't see them, it just feels wrong. I can't explain it. It's like losing sight of home base. Like I have a compass inside, but it points west instead of north." I stopped short and wished I hadn't said all that. "There. Is that better?"

He leaned back with a sigh, his head on my thigh, and looked up at me. "Yes. That did help. You were right."

"Told you."

"Thanks."

But he didn't move. His eyes had closed, and he seemed to be half asleep.

His head was practically in my lap. It didn't seem to faze him, but it felt incredibly intimate to me. Suddenly, my heart was racing and my mouth was dry. I couldn't take my eyes off of him. Nothing else existed at that moment. I had never seen anything as ruggedly beautiful as him. His jaw was strong and square, and at least a day's worth of dark stubble covered his cheeks. His lips were soft and full. He never wore sunglasses, and there were small squint lines around his eyes, slightly pale against his tan face. His lashes weren't long, but they were thick and jet black.

I could have looked at him all night. I was aware of some strange feeling which seemed to suffuse my entire being. It was overwhelming—almost painful yet not unpleasant. I felt that I must certainly be glowing with it. This current that was flowing through me felt like a fever through my skin. Surely he could feel it where his head was touching my thigh. How could he be so close to me, touching me, and not sense what I was feeling? I had always been attracted to him. I had always enjoyed spending time with him. But I realized at that moment that at some point over the past few weeks, it had become something more.

I loved him.

It was a painful realization—so painful that it took my breath away—discovering that I was totally in love with this man who would never love me back.

I wanted nothing more than to kiss him and was both annoyed and relieved that I could not possibly do it from where I sat. I knew I would not have been able to stop myself otherwise. My hand moved of its own volition and came to rest along his cheek, my fingertips just touching his jaw. His eyes drifted open, and he looked up at me, his green-in-gray eyes looking into mine, and I knew he could see it in my eyes. There was no way he could look at me at that moment and not know what I was feeling.

He slowly put his hand up, grabbed my fingers, and pulled them away from his cheek. He didn't let go of my hand. His voice was very quiet but very gentle when he asked, "Are you sure you're not making a pass at me?"

I couldn't even answer at first. It certainly had not been my intention at the beginning, but at that moment, I didn't think I could bear to not have him.

71

"Would it work?" My voice was barely more than a whisper.

He hesitated for a second, but whether it was because he was unsure of the answer or because he knew I wasn't going to like his answer, I didn't know. But then, just slightly, he shook his head. "No."

It was the answer I expected, and yet I couldn't believe how much it hurt. I couldn't look at him anymore. I had to close my eyes, had to remind myself to take a single, shaking breath. I could barely speak around the sudden lump in my throat. "I guess it doesn't matter then, does it?"

I started to pull away, but his hand, still holding my fingers, suddenly gripped tight. "Jared?" When I looked back down at him, he said, "Do you want me to leave?"

The question surprised me, and I answered honestly. "No. Not at all." I pulled my hand away from his and stood up, not facing him, one hand over my eyes. "Matt, I...." I wasn't sure what I was going to say, but what came out was, "I'm sorry."

"Don't be." He said it with such gentle honesty, and it made me feel a little better. It was a relief to know that at least my desire for him would not cost me his friendship. But I still couldn't look at him. Out of the corner of my eyes, I saw him get up and put his shirt back on. He came over and put his hand on my shoulder, waiting until I finally looked up at his face. He gave me an almost-smile and said, "Come on. Let's go make those nachos."

WE SPENT the last Sunday of August on my couch watching football. We were as excited as kids on Christmas to have the season under way. For the morning game we cheered for the same team, but for the afternoon game we were cheering against each other. I had never experienced such a perfect feeling of camaraderie. We laughed at each other and insulted each other and occasionally threw things at one another and drank too much beer. And near the end, he sighed happily, leaned back next to me on the couch, and said, "I'm definitely coming here every Sunday."

"Don't forget there's football on Mondays too."

CHAPTER 14

I RIDE my bike to and from work year 'round, resorting to my car only when there's snow on the ground. I don't know for sure, but I've always suspected that it's the only reason I've managed to stay thin. Most of the time I enjoy it but not today. We were having one of our late afternoon thunderstorms, very common for Colorado in early September. The rain was chilly, and visibility was limited. The worst part was that I had originally planned to stop at the store on the way home since there was nothing edible in my house. But with the rain, I found all I really wanted to do was get home and get dry.

Maybe Matt would come by tonight, and we could order a pizza.

I had my head down and was pedaling down the sidewalk as fast as I could when a car hit me. It was coming out of a driveway, moving slow, which is probably what saved me. The driver was talking on his cell phone, not paying attention—just like Lizzy always predicted. I hoped she would be happy.

He hit me on my left side. I felt the front of the hood hit my head, and then I flew out into the street. Later, I would realize how lucky I was that no cars were coming. I slid a few feet across the asphalt on my right side before coming to a stop in the middle of the street.

"Oh shit, I'm so sorry! I wasn't looking! Are you hurt?" The driver was already out of his car and leaning over me. I recognized him from around town. His name was Jason. Other than that I didn't know anything about him.

"I think I'm okay." Actually, I had no idea. I was stunned and trying to survey the damage. Nothing hurt yet, but that didn't mean anything.

"I think I better take you to the hospital."

When I looked up at him, I was surprised to see how scared he looked.

"I think I'm okay." I was actually more worried about the state of my bike.

"You're bleeding." Jason pointed toward my left ear.

I put my hand against my head, and it came away covered in blood which was quickly washed away again by the rain. "Oh shit." I realized there was blood on my shirt and in the rainy water on the street.

Jason was starting to panic now. "Let me take you to the hospital."

The pain was starting to come now too. It was either let him take me or wait here for cops and an ambulance. I got in his car.

"THE wound on your head looks worse than it actually is," the doctor told me. "Of course, if you had been wearing a helmet, you would be home by now with only a few bumps and bruises instead of bleeding in my emergency room." I knew he was right. Worse than that, I knew that Lizzy, Brian, and my mom were all going to give me the same lecture at least a hundred times over the next few days. "There's no sign of concussion, so once we've got your

75

wounds clean and bandaged, you'll be able to go home. Do you have somebody you can call to pick you up?"

"Yes."

"Good. I'm going to get you some Oxycodone—"

"I hate that stuff. It makes me itchy."

"That's a fairly common side effect. Would you prefer Vicodin?"

"Definitely."

"I'm going to give you a little bit now, plus I'll send you home with a pretty heavy dose to take before bed. But only for tonight. You'll probably be pretty sore tomorrow but try to make do with over-the-counter pain relievers."

"You bet." Everything was definitely starting to hurt, and I knew it was only going to get worse.

They gave me the first round of drugs and then closed the wound on my left temple with something that smelled suspiciously like super glue. Besides being covered with blood, my shirt had been shredded by my skid on the asphalt. They threw it away, painfully cleaned the giant patch of road rash on my right side, spread some kind of goo all over it and bandaged it, and then gave me a blue scrub shirt to wear home.

Cops were in and out, asking me questions. Matt apparently was not on duty. Jason gave me his insurance information and promised to bring my bike by my house the next day. It seemed to go on forever. It was almost nine o'clock when the doctor finally brought me the second dose of Vicodin. "You can take these in a couple of hours," he said as he handed them to me. I nodded even though I knew I wouldn't wait that long. He handed me a cordless phone. "Call your ride now. I'll want to talk to them before you leave."

I took the pills as soon as he left the room and thought about who to call. Lizzy would be a wreck, crying and trying to baby me. Brian would yell about me being an idiot. Mom would cry and give me a lecture on the same topic.

I called Matt.

"Hey Jared," he said when he picked up. "Where the hell are you? I went by your house."

"I'm at the hospital. Can you come get me?"

"Are you okay? What happened?" he asked with genuine alarm.

"I got hit by a car, but—"

Of course he didn't let me finish. "What! Jesus, Jared, are you okay?"

"I'm fine. But they won't let me go unless I have a ride home."

"I'll be there in five minutes."

When Matt got there, the doctor took him into the hallway, and they talked for a while. By the time we got in the car, I was already feeling better.

"Please don't lecture me," I said as we got in the car. "Just let it wait until morning."

"Okay." He said it like it hadn't even occurred to him. I could have kissed him.

By the time we got to my house, I was dead on my feet. Between the Vicodin and the adrenaline crash, I felt like I could barely put one foot in front of the other. I sat down on the couch, leaned back and closed my eyes. I felt him sit down next to me. Nothing happened for a minute. Or maybe it was an hour.

The whole world was soft around the edges, not quite tangible. I knew I was in pain, but I was drifting on top of it, buoyed by the drugs, and comfortable back in my own home. I might have slept for a bit. I couldn't be sure. At some point, I became aware of him again at my side, and then a feather-light touch near my temple, where the cut was. I cracked my eyes open a tiny bit. He was next to me but facing me, one leg tucked under him, looking at the cut on my head. His fingers were carefully pushing my hair back out of the way. My eyes closed again, and I drifted for a while, feeling his fingers moving in my hair. My head still hurt, but his light touch felt nice.

"Jesus, Jared." Matt said, and it was not his usual bantering voice. It was almost a whisper, very strained, and it surprised me. My eyes opened a tiny bit. He was leaning close, looking at me, and the expression on his face was one I had never seen before. His eyebrows were down a little bit, and his eyes, not very far away from my own, were dark and troubled. His fingers seemed to still be moving in my hair, against my scalp, almost like a caress, but my addled brain wasn't sure. "You could have died."

Even in my drugged state, I was surprised by how much raw emotion I could hear in those four words. I had no idea what to say, but what came out of my mouth was, "I'm okay."

His eyes closed. His fingers were still in my hair but not moving anymore. "Thank God." I couldn't get my brain to work. Something about this was strange and wrong, but I couldn't figure out what it was. He finally opened his eyes, and I must have looked confused, because he suddenly smiled at me a little bit and said, "Just how much Vicodin did they give you?"

"Enough." I could easily have slept there the rest of the night and was especially reluctant to move away from where his fingers were tangled in my hair, just barely touching my head.

He shook his head at me, still smiling a little, and said, "Come on. Time for bed."

He stood up, pulled me off the couch, and pushed me toward my bedroom. Once we got there, he said, "Do you have any sweats that might fit me?"

That confused me, but I pointed to a drawer.

"Okay." He started digging through the drawer. He glanced back over and raised his eyebrow at me in amusement. "Jared, I'm not going to undress you," he said lightly. "You'll have to do that yourself."

I hadn't actually realized that's what I was supposed to be doing. I obediently took off my shoes and socks and pants, and I sat down on the bed. I wasn't sure what to do next.

Matt came over and looked down at me with the pseudo-smile. "Close enough." He pulled the hospital shirt off of me. His expression darkened again, that strange look I didn't recognize, when he saw the bruises and giant bandage on my side. Then he pushed me gently backward on the bed. I turned onto my uninjured side and snuggled down into my bed with relief. He pulled the blankets up over me. When was the last time somebody had tucked me in? My eyes were already closed, and I was drifting again. Some time later, the mattress creaked. I opened my eyes a little. The room was dark, but I could still see him, wearing a pair of my sweats, getting into the other side of the bed.

"You're sleeping here?" I managed to ask, although I seemed to be slurring my words a little.

"I'm not leaving you alone tonight. The doctor said to call right away if you started vomiting."

"Will you be here when I wake up?" I didn't know why that mattered, but some part of my brain apparently wanted to know.

I felt his hand wrap tight around my wrist. "I promise."

I WOKE up in the morning to the smell of bacon cooking. I was ravenously hungry, my whole body hurt, my mouth tasted terrible, and my head was pounding. I made it into the bathroom, emptied my bladder, brushed my teeth, and started cleaning up. Between the road rash and the superglue, a shower wasn't even an option. The left side of my face had a massive bruise from my temple to my jaw. Yep, my mom was definitely going to freak out. I would have preferred being hit by another car to facing her.

My memory of the evening after leaving the hospital was a blur of hazy images: pain, but also a light touch on my temple, a hand wrapped around my wrist in the dark. Did he really sleep in my bed with me? *Talk about opportunity wasted,* I thought as I took two each of Tylenol and ibuprofen.

"How do you feel?" he asked as I came into the kitchen and sat down at the breakfast bar.

"Like I was hit by a Mack truck."

"Nope." He put a plate of bacon, eggs, and toast in front of me. "Just a Toyota Land Cruiser." A glass of milk and a cup of coffee came next. It occurred to me that, with the exception of the coffee, none of this food had been in my house. He must have gone out early to get it.

"Holy shit, I'm hungry!"

"You had Vicodin for dinner."

"That explains it." I dug in.

"I called Lizzy and told her you would be late."

I groaned as I thought about what Lizzy was going to say about the whole thing. "Did you tell her what happened?"

"No." He sounded amused.

"You want me to get the full brunt of her freaking out when I tell her, don't you?"

"Exactly." His eyes were crinkled at the corners, almost laughing. "Plus, I could tell she was dying to know why I was calling from your house at seven thirty in the morning. I thought it would be fun to let her imagination run wild." That certainly would get Lizzy's bees buzzing, and I had to laugh. "Mind if I use the shower?" he asked.

"Help yourself." I was already most of the way through the plate of food. He didn't head for the shower though. He stood looking at me like he had something to say but didn't know how. It made me self-conscious enough that I stopped eating and looked up at him. "What?"

He walked over and stood next to me at the counter. For a minute, he didn't move. I waited. I was expecting the lecture to start. But then he leaned toward me, put one hand under my hair on the back of my neck, pulled me toward him, and buried his face in my hair. He was shaking. He took one ragged breath, and then his lips brushed my ear when he whispered, "Don't ever scare me like that again."

I was stunned. I knew I was his only real friend in town, but I was still surprised at how shaken up he seemed to be. Suddenly I remembered his look from the night before, that strange expression I had never seen before. I remembered the emotion in his voice when he said I could have died. I was overwhelmingly touched by how much he cared about me. It was hard to make my throat work, but I managed to say, "I'll do my best."

"Good." He let go of me, grabbed my helmet off of the counter, and shoved it into my stomach, hard enough to make me wince.

"From now on," he said. It did not sound like a request.

My first instinct was to protest, but when I looked back up, I saw that look again. The one from last night. Could I really deny him anything? The answer was simple: no. I loved him too much.

"I promise."

CHAPTER 15

TRUE to form, my family freaked out about the accident, but once they learned that Matt had made me promise to wear my helmet, they let it go. Mom called it a "blessing in disguise." I tried not to roll my eyes when she said it. I was also relieved to find out that my bike wasn't badly damaged. And so within a matter of days, the incident was, for the most part, forgotten. And if I wondered a little about Matt's strange display of affection, I said nothing.

"You look like hell!" I had just opened my front door to find Matt leaning on the doorframe. I wasn't sure why he even bothered knocking anymore. He looked like he might have fallen asleep there if I had taken any longer getting to the door.

"I just pulled a double shift. I'm exhausted." He came in and threw himself onto the couch. "Have you bought any food yet? I'm starving."

"You know I haven't. But I'm hungry too. Come on, let's go out. My treat."

He groaned. "Where we gonna go?"

"Mamacita's?"

"No. Cherie might be there."

"Is that a problem?"

"Yes."

"Since when?"

"Since I quit seeing her three weeks ago."

That surprised me, but I let it go. "Okay then. How about Tony's?"

"No. We can't go there either."

"Why not?"

"That blonde girl—I forgot her name. She's always giving me her phone number."

"Maybe it's her night off?"

"If it is, then that other one will be there. The one that wears too much of that stinky hippie perfume. She practically sat in my lap last time."

I was starting to grin despite myself.

"Is there any restaurant in town that we *can* go to?"

"No!" He groaned.

"Must be tough being the town's most eligible bachelor." I was having a hard time not laughing.

"I'm glad you find it so amusing."

"And you're not interested in any of them?"

He was looking right at me. He was so tired; all his defenses were down, and I knew he meant it when he said, "No. I would rather be here." God, that was good to hear, but I tried to keep my tone casual.

"You think if you hang out with the gay guy long enough, they'll finally start to leave you alone?"

"That would certainly be an added bonus." His eyes were closed now, his breathing starting to slow.

"It doesn't seem to be working so far."

"Jared, shut up and order a pizza."

When the pizza arrived, I brought out a couple of beers and flipped on the TV. He was still quiet and strangely pensive. I checked the on-screen TV Guide. "We gotta sit through the last forty minutes of *The Breakfast Club*, but then *Wrath of Khan* starts."

"Whatever."

I wasn't sure how to handle this side of him. Usually he was so solid, but tonight it felt like he was lost. Like he was waiting for somebody to lead him home. He had hardly eaten any pizza although he was on his third beer.

"Are you working tomorrow?" I asked.

"Day off."

"Let's go for a ride. We haven't been up in a couple of weeks."

He brightened up a little. "Sure. I could use the exercise."

He was slouched down, his long legs stretched out in front of him. His head was tilted back, and his arms were stretched out along the back of the couch so that one hand was resting behind my head. Half the time his eyes were closed, and I thought he was drifting in and out of sleep. We sat in silence for a while, and then he said suddenly, "I hate this movie."

"Because it's sentimental crap or because nothing gets blown up?" It was supposed to be a joke, but I don't think he even heard me.

"None of them even know who they are. They're just acting out their roles. Being what their parents made them. Always trying to be what's expected. It's exhausting."

Somehow I didn't think he was only talking about the movie.

"I think I envy you," he said. "You don't ever get tired, do you? You don't care what they expect."

"Whose expectations are you worried about, Matt?"

"Nobody's. Everybody's. Fuck, I don't even know what I'm talking about. I'm so tired." His eyes were closed again. "Don't listen to me."

I was pretty sure he had fallen asleep. I sat there, feet up on the coffee table, staring at the movie without seeing it, wondering what had happened to put him in this mood. Then I felt a small tug on the back of my head. Then another. I realized it was his hand. He was feeling my hair, gently pulling on my curls.

"Did something happen today, Matt?" He was watching his own fingers as they played in my hair, but I don't think he was really seeing them. It was possible he hadn't quite realized he was doing it. It felt nice, and I stayed perfectly still. I was afraid if I moved an inch, he would stop. "Is there something going on at work?"

The tug on my hair stopped. His jaw clenched, and I knew I had hit on something.

"No."

"I know you're lying."

There was no answer for a minute, but then that gentle pull on my hair started again.

"They're having a picnic. You know, a department thing, everybody bringing their families."

He stopped, but I knew there was more. "And you don't have a family?"

"That's not the problem." He sighed and took a deep breath like he was going to tell me. Then he stopped short, shaking his head. "Never mind." He stopped playing with my hair and looked back at the TV like the subject was closed.

"Then what *is* the problem?"

It took him a while to decide to answer, but he finally said in a quiet voice, "They asked me if I was going to bring a guest. And I mentioned you."

I was shocked. "You shouldn't have done that."

"No shit."

"What did they say?"

"They told me 'boyfriends' aren't allowed." He sighed again. "I know you warned me. I know I should have seen it coming. But we're friends, right?" He didn't wait for me to answer. "I'm not allowed to have a friend? And what if it *was* more?" I just about choked on my beer when he said that, but he didn't seem to notice. "Why is it their business? They expect me to go sit at their fucking picnic—alone—and watch them with their happy fucking little families, and I'm supposed to pretend like the one person in this town I give a damn about doesn't even exist?"

"Uh...." I couldn't really think of anything to say to that. I couldn't believe that he had said any of it and was pretty sure he wouldn't have on any normal day. But it didn't matter. He was still talking, and the pull on the back of my head had resumed.

"And *then* my parents called. Talk about great timing. My mom's all in a lather because her sister has a billion grandkids and she has none. My dad was drunk, which is nothing new, and he's talking about duty. I don't know if he means being something more than a cop, or if he means getting married and settling down. Both, I guess. And all I can think about is how much I wish I had a brother or a sister, so they could shift some of their expectations to somebody other than me." The gentle tug on the back of my head continued. "Everybody wants something, and everybody expects something. They never ask how I'm doing or if I'm happy. They don't ask what I want."

"And what do you want?"

86

His hand and head both fell back onto the back of the couch. His eyes were on the ceiling. "I wish I knew."

I wasn't sure what to say to that. I turned back to the TV, and after a minute, the gentle tug on my curls resumed.

"Jared, what do you want?" His voice was quiet, and when I looked over, his grey eyes locked on mine. "Tell me what *you're* expecting."

My heart skipped a beat. Was he asking how I felt about him? I could tell him that I had no expectations, and that was certainly true. But as to what I wanted, that was simple. I wanted him. But I was pretty sure he already knew that, and I didn't think verbalizing it would help anything. So instead I said, "I'm expecting to kick your ass on the trail tomorrow."

And just barely, he smiled. "Then I better get some sleep."

"Are you okay to drive home?"

"I'm not even gonna try." And two minutes later, he was sound asleep.

BY THE time I got up, Matt had already showered, gone out for donuts, and made coffee. His strange mood seemed forgotten as he shoved me out the door.

We had a great ride. I had one spectacular crash on the way up, resulting in two skinned knees and an oozing abrasion that ran from my shoulder to my elbow. Before I could even get up, I heard what could only be described as maniacal laughter. The part of my brain that wasn't thinking about how much pain I was in wondered who was laughing, because I had certainly never heard anything like that come out of Matt's mouth. And then, before I knew what was happening, he jumped on me and pinned me to the ground. I'm close to six feet, but I'm not exactly a big guy. Matt outweighed me by twenty to thirty pounds, and he had no trouble holding me down.

"My God, you're heavy! What the hell are you doing?"

His body was all muscle and sweat, and his eyes were flashing green as he laughed down at me. "Rubbing dirt on it!" And he proceeded to grab a handful of it and smear it all over my arm. It hurt like hell, but at the same time, it was strangely erotic, having him on top of me like that, and it left me feeling slightly aroused and incredibly off balance.

When we reached the top of the trail, we took off our helmets, dropped our bikes, and stood on the summit, looking down at the valley below us. The sun was golden, the sky brilliant blue. The light breeze was filled with the smell of the evergreens around us. The aspens were changing, making bright patches of amber, orange, and magenta within the green. It was a perfect moment, standing there next to him, covered in sweat and dirt and blood, seeing the glory of the Rocky Mountains around us.

I turned to look at him, to see if he felt it too, and found that he wasn't seeing it at all. He was looking at me. His head was cocked a little to the side, like something was puzzling him, and he was smiling a little. But the thing that really startled me was his eyes. If I had ever imagined him looking at me like that, it had only been in my sweetest dreams.

He reached up, over my shoulder to my hair. Was the whole world in slow motion? I felt like I couldn't even breathe. There was a tug, and I realized he had pulled the rubber band free. Then his fingers were pushing up against my scalp and into my hair. My breath caught in my throat, and my eyes closed. I don't know how long we stood like that. It felt like forever. It felt like only a heartbeat.

"Lizzy's wrong. You definitely shouldn't cut it."

His hand was gone, and when I opened my eyes, he was heading back to his bike. But he gave me his brilliant smile—would

I ever get used to seeing it?—when he turned to look at me. "Last one down pays for dinner."

"ALL right, Jared! Spill!"

I turned to see Lizzy grinning at me, her blue eyes practically glowing with mischievous anticipation.

"I don't know what you're talking about."

"Don't give me that. You can't wander around here all day with your head in the clouds and a perma-grin on your face and expect me to believe that there's *nothing* going on. So—spill!"

I knew she was right. I felt like I had been floating a foot above ground all day.

"I'm just having a good day."

"It's Matt, isn't it?"

"Yes. Well, no. Not exactly."

"What is it then, *exactly*?"

I didn't know what to say, but I knew my ridiculous grin was bigger than ever.

"Please tell me he's finally coming around?"

"Well, I don't want to get your hopes up too high"—or my own—"but I actually think there's a ghost of chance."

She squealed and threw her arms around my neck. She had caught me a little off guard. One arm was pinned to my side by her round belly, and her hair was in my mouth. "That's so great, Jared!"

The bell over the door rang, and Matt walked in. "What are you two so happy about?"

I knew my cheeks were bright red, but Lizzy was smooth as

always. "Jared was just telling me that he plans to baby sit for us one night a week after the baby is born so that Brian and I can go out. Isn't that nice of him?" Did I say smooth? I don't think that quite covers it. She had managed to answer him without embarrassing me and had secured herself a weekly date night all in one stroke. You had to admire her. "So Matt, did Jared tell you about his birthday?"

"No." He looked at me expectantly.

"It's still two weeks away," I told him.

"It's September twenty-first," Lizzy said. "I'm making dinner. You'll come, right?"

He looked right at me and said, "Wouldn't miss it."

CHAPTER 16

DURING the two weeks leading up to my birthday, my confusion continued to grow. Matt spent every single evening at my house. He slept on my couch as often as he went home, although he was always gone by the time I dragged my lazy ass out of bed in the morning. He even bought a toothbrush to keep at my house. I tried to tell myself it was only because he didn't want to go home to his sterile, empty apartment. I mostly believed it. But was I imagining that he was watching me more, touching me when he didn't need to? Many nights as we watched TV on my couch, I would feel that gentle tug on the back of my head. It was a form of torture, but one that I looked forward to every day.

Matt worked on my birthday but was done at five. He picked me up, and we went to Lizzy's house for dinner.

It was a strange night. As the hours passed, he was moving closer, a heat burning in his eyes that I had seen before, in other men's eyes, but not for a long time. It seemed like he couldn't stop touching me. Taken individually, they were just casual touches on my arm, or my shoulder, or my back. He touched my hair a lot too. It was feeling less casual by the minute. With anybody else, I would have known exactly what it meant. With him, I had no idea.

Even my family noticed. I saw Mom's small, knowing smile and Brian's uneasy bemusement. And how could I miss Lizzy's ear-to-ear grin or the goofy thumbs-up she gave me behind his back? But he still seemed to be blind to what he was doing. I had been partially erect all night and hoping that nobody had noticed.

At the end of the night, Lizzy declared us both unfit to drive and gave us a ride back to my house. By the time we pulled up in front of my house, my head was spinning. I had heard that term before but had never really understood it until now.

I wasn't sure what to expect. Probably he would just drink another beer and then crash on my couch. But part of me knew that we were on a precipice, looking down. We either had to turn around and walk away or take a deep breath and jump. My hands were shaking so much that it took me three tries to get the key in the lock. He was contentedly humming behind me, swaying on his feet a little, and I don't think he noticed.

I finally got us inside and made a break for the kitchen, calling over my shoulder, "I'll get us something to drink." I got glasses out of the cabinet and beers out of the fridge, took an ice tray out of the freezer, and stood there, staring down at them, not really knowing what I was going to do next. Normally I would just grab two bottles of beer out of the fridge, but I was flustered and trying desperately to buy enough time to regain some equilibrium. I didn't hear him come in. Just suddenly felt him behind me, his hands on my waist. It made me a little breathless, feeling him so big and solid against my back. Didn't he know what he was doing to me?

But his voice in my ear wasn't the sexy drawl of a lover. It was the same casual, bantering voice he always used. "What are you doing in here?" He leaned against me harder as he reached out with one hand and picked up one of the bottles. "Who ordered beer on the rocks?" I couldn't see his face, but I knew he had one eyebrow cocked.

"I'm, uh, I'm not sure." I was stammering like an idiot, trying to think about football or mountain bikes or anything but how close he was. He put the beer down, and his weight against my back lessened some, but his left hand was back on my waist. His right hand slid up and over to rest on my stomach, and my breath caught in my throat.

"Hey," he actually sounded a little concerned now. "Are you okay? You're shaking."

I laughed nervously. "No kidding?"

"No kidding. What's wrong?"

I took a deep breath and said, "Matt, you may not realize it, but you're sending me some seriously mixed signals here. I'm not quite sure how you want me to react."

"What do you mean?" And man, that really did sound like genuine confusion in his voice. But he still hadn't moved.

"I mean this, Matt. The way you're touching me."

"Oh." I knew without looking that his cheeks were turning red. "Do you want me to stop?"

"No, I don't *want* you to stop. But, I think maybe you should."

"What? Why?" Confused. But then as realization hit, "*Oh!*" But he didn't move. A second passed, and then his hand moved a little higher, toward my chest. His weight against my back increased, and his voice had gone low and husky when he said in my ear, "Am I turning you on?"

"God, yes, you're turning me on!" It came out a little harsh, but I was relieved to get it out. "Is that what you want?"

He froze for a minute, and his breath in my ear was a little bit shaky. "I don't really know." Another shaky breath and his hands fell away, and I felt him step back. "I'm sorry. I really didn't mean to." But when I turned around, I realized he had only taken a half-step back. He was only a foot away from me. His cheeks were flushed, and he was obviously as shaken as I was.

For a minute, neither of us moved. I was trying to catch my

93

breath and convince my cock that there was nothing of interest going on. It wasn't listening. My whole body was shaking, and my voice came out raspy. "Okay, well—"

I stopped short when he suddenly stepped forward again. My back was against the counter. My fingers had a death grip on its edge. He was so close. He was looking at me, frowning, his head cocked a little to the side like he was trying to figure something out. Like I was some kind of puzzle that he almost had the answer to. Then, slowly, he put both hands on the countertop, one on either side of me, pinning me in. "Matt?" It came out barely a whisper.

I could definitely see the green in his eyes tonight. They were full of surprise and confusion, but there was something else there too. "I guess I just want to touch you." One hand came off the counter, onto my hip. "I think"—he sounded amazed—"I really like touching you." Now his hand was sliding up my arm. His lips were only an inch away from mine. My whole body felt electric, like every nerve was straining toward him. "Is it okay if I touch you?"

I gave up, closed my eyes, relaxed against his tall, strong body, and thought about nothing but how good his hand felt. "Yes."

He put his hand in my hair, pulling lightly on the curls. For a moment I only felt fingers moving through my hair. Then he grabbed a handful of it and pulled my head back so that my neck was exposed. He leaned over and put his lips against my neck. Soft lips and rough stubble brushed up to my jaw and moved toward my ear. I was sure my heart was going to pound its way right out of my chest. Or that my cock was going to burst through the buttons on my jeans. His lips brushed my ear, and he whispered, "I just want to touch you a little more."

I wanted to tell him that he never had to stop, but I couldn't speak. I was afraid that if I touched him back, the spell would somehow be broken. But I reached out and put one hand on his flat stomach. He responded by wrapping his other arm around my waist. His tongue touched my ear. His cheek was like sandpaper against my own. I pulled up his shirt, slid my hands underneath, and ran them up his back. I felt the hard muscles there jump under my fingers, and he made a little moan against my neck that went straight to my groin.

I hadn't thought there was any space left between us, but he managed to push closer. The entire length of my body was against his. His arms were tight around me, one hand wandering up and down my back, the other still tangled in my curls. I felt his lips on my neck. Not just brushing over the skin, like before. He was really kissing me now, nipping at my neck, his tongue flicking over my pounding pulse. Then both of his hands were on my hips, pulling my groin harder against his, and I felt his erection grinding against my own.

I heard myself moan, or maybe it was more of a whimper. Whatever it was, he obviously liked it, because the gentle nibbles on my neck suddenly became something much more insistent. He put both hands into my hair. All of his weight was against me now, holding me against the counter. He was pulling harder on my hair, pushing his hips into mine, and whatever he was doing to my neck was bordering on painful, but I definitely didn't want it to stop.

It took me a couple of tries, but I finally managed to whisper, "Do you want to go in the bedroom?"

Me and my big mouth.

He froze, a breathing statue with both hands still tangled in my hair, and his lips still warm against my neck. "Matt?"

And then he let me go. Before I knew it, he was on the other side of the room. I was reeling. I felt like half of my body had just been ripped away.

"Matt?"

He sat down on one of the bar stools with his elbows on his knees and his head in his hands. "Oh my God. What just happened? What the hell just happened?" He made a sound that might have been a laugh… or a sob. "I don't know what's happening to me. I think I'm losing my fucking mind."

I took a step toward him and reached out my hand.

"Don't touch me!" It came out as a snarl.

He might as well have punched me, it hurt so much.

"Matt, it's okay."

"It is most definitely not okay! Oh my God, this is *not* okay. I wanted to…. How could I want that? How can I want you like this?"

"Matt, I want you too. I have for a long time. There's nothing wrong with that."

His only response was to shake his head in his hands.

"Matt, I know what you've told me. But be honest with me. This can't be the first time you've been attracted to another guy."

He was silent so long I was starting to think I had taken a serious misstep. But then, very quietly, he said, "You're right. I've been attracted to other men before. Not many, but a few. But not like this. Nothing *ever* like this." He took a deep, shuddering breath. "It was always just a physical reaction, and I was able to just ignore it. Just tell myself no. Tell myself that it was wrong."

He looked up at me, and the pain and confusion in his eyes was enough to break my heart. "Whatever this is with me and you, it's so much more, and I can't make it go away."

How could those words make me so happy while hurting so much at the same time? "Matt, why does it have to go away?"

"I'm so confused, Jared. Even now, all I can think about is how much I want to touch you. And I just have no idea what to do about it."

I went to him. Sitting on the stool, he was actually a little shorter than me. His eyes were wary as I approached, but he didn't stop me. I stepped between his knees, took his face in my hands, and looked into his eyes.

"I do, Matt. I know exactly what to do about it. Come in the bedroom with me and let me show you what we can do about it." I leaned in and kissed him, just barely brushing my lips against his. "Please, Matt? Trust me. Please don't turn away from this."

There were tears on his cheeks. "But it's wrong."

"You know I don't believe that. I don't see how it can be wrong." His eyes were closed, and when I kissed the corner of his mouth, I heard his breath catch in his throat. "Does this feel wrong to you?" I kissed the tears from one cheek. "Because it doesn't feel wrong to me." The other cheek. "Nothing in my life has ever felt so right." I pulled back and waited until he opened his eyes and looked into mine. "I love you, Matt. How can that be wrong? How can love be wrong?"

But it was too much. When I said that word, the doors slammed shut. He reached up and took my wrists, carefully pulled my hands from his face, shaking his head. He stood up, gently pushing me back away from him as he did.

"I have to go."

"Matt. Please don't. Please don't walk away from this."

But he didn't even look back.

I WAS sitting in the shop, contemplating a crack in the countertop. To be honest, I had been contemplating that crack for over an hour. A couple of people had come in, but I let Ringo deal with them. I did make sure I kept my hand over the marks on my neck while they were in the store. No need to give the town gossips something else to talk about. I couldn't remember ever being so depressed over hickeys before.

97

I heard Lizzy come in the back door and walk up to me. Then she laughed. "Oh my God, look at your neck! Looks like somebody had one hell of a birthday."

But when I looked up at her, she must have seen the pain in my eyes right away. Her face fell and she dropped onto the stool next to me. "What happened?"

"I don't want to talk about it."

"Oh Jared. After yesterday, the way he was watching you and touching you, I was just sure...."

"Still don't want to talk about it."

"Did the two of you have a fight?"

"Not exactly."

"Did you break up?"

"Lizzy, we would have had to be together in order for us to break up."

"Then what?"

So I told her. And the sympathy in her blue eyes was almost the worst part of it.

She hugged me despite her bulging belly. "I'm sure he'll come around. He's obviously as crazy about you as you are about him. Just give him some time."

But I couldn't believe her.

CHAPTER 17

I CALLED him a few times over the next week or two, but he never answered. I left messages.

The first time, three days after my birthday, I tried to sound casual. "Matt, it's okay. We both had a lot to drink." I didn't think that had anything to do with what had happened, but I was willing to give him that as an excuse if it would help. "It doesn't matter. Call me."

Three days after that, I was starting to feel desperately lost. "Matt, you don't have to avoid me. Nothing happened. Let's just forget it. See you on Sunday, okay?"

And when he didn't show up to watch football on Sunday, I called again. I had carefully thought out what I was going to say after the beep—something glib about his Chiefs losing to the Raiders. But for some reason, the words died on my tongue. All I managed to say was, "Matt, I miss you."

I didn't call again after that.

The next few weeks were miserable. Matt continued to avoid me. And worst of all, he started dating Cherie. Not just sleeping with her, like he had over the summer, but actually dating.

I knew what he was doing. He was trying to convince himself

99

that he could be happy with a woman. He was telling himself that his feelings for me were nothing more than the result of having spent too much time together and that if he just spent more time with Cherie, he could transfer those feelings to her. I didn't think it would work, and yet I was terrified that it would.

I couldn't believe how lonely I was. I tried to comfort myself with the thought that my life was now just as it had been for years before he arrived. It hadn't seemed that bad back then. But now I felt crushed. My house felt like a graveyard. Every time the door opened in the shop, I hoped it was him, but it never was. Every evening, I hoped he would knock on the door. Even football wasn't as much fun. The few Sundays we had spent together watching it, our perfect companionship, taunted me as I sat by myself, watching the games. Lizzy and Brian invited me over, of course, and I went once or twice, but instead of cheering me up, it only served to depress Lizzy, so I quit going.

"He's not even happy," she told me one day. "Brian and I saw them when we went out to dinner, and he looked miserable."

And the worst part was that I thought she was right. The times I had seen him, he did look miserable. Even his pseudo-smile hadn't been there.

"Why are you telling me this, Lizzy?"

"I think he misses you as much as you miss him. Why don't you call him?"

"No."

"Jared—"

"No!" I stopped short. Lizzy didn't deserve for me to snap at her. She just wanted me to be happy. But if there was one thing I knew, it was that I couldn't be the one to make the next move. He was the one who couldn't face his feelings or what they meant. The only thing I could do was wait and hope.

"HEY, Jared? Can I ask a favor?" Ringo said one day in early October as we were unpacking cases of motor oil.

"What's up?"

"Do you think that you could tutor me again?"

"With math?"

"Yes. I'm taking calculus now, and it's kicking my ass."

"Of course." It was depressing how much I was suddenly looking forward to spending time with Ringo. Talk about a lame social life.

"And you know physics too?"

"That's what my degree's in. You need help with that too?"

"If it's okay. Can I come by your house to do it? I feel bad taking up time here at the shop."

"What about your dad?"

"I think it will be okay. I mean, he was really glad that you helped me last spring. And I told him that he needs to trust people. And he needs to trust me. I'll be eighteen soon. I'm not a kid, and I'm not stupid." He stopped and looked embarrassed. "Except at math and physics, I guess."

"You're not stupid. My house is fine."

We arranged for him to come by the house on Tuesday and Thursday evenings.

The first week, Ringo came alone. The second week, he showed up with a girl.

"This is my girlfriend, Julie." She was cute, a little heavy set, with dark hair and freckles she tried to cover with makeup. "Do you

101

think you can tutor us both?"

And so I had two students that week. I ordered pizza and was glad to have the company, even if it was just two teenagers who couldn't figure out integration.

I was surprised to find that Julie had the same bad habit that Ringo had started out with.

"Why do you want to replace the variable with numbers already?"

"That's how you simplify."

"Variables are easy. Numbers complicate things. Wait until the end. Here," I pointed to the physics problem she was working on. "Look at this one. What do you know about F?"

"Force equals mass times acceleration."

"Right. So what if we put 'M times A' in place of F in this equation?"

"But we're supposed to be solving for F!"

"Yes, but what do you see on the other side of the equation?"

She was looking, and I saw the light start to come on. "M and A." I watched her process that. And then she was furiously scratching away with her pencil, talking as she went. "I can eliminate M, and then, I have 2A, but then...." *scratch, scratch, scratch* "Now I have A!"

"Right. And you already had M—"

"So now I just multiply them, and I get F!"

"Exactly."

"It's like a puzzle!" Her eyes were bright with excitement.

"That's one way of viewing it, yes."

And the look of understanding and accomplishment on her

face was a remarkable balm for the ache in my heart.

It didn't stop there. The next week, they brought another girl. And then she brought her boyfriend. By the end of the month, I had ten different students who would drop by for help in math or physics on Tuesdays and Thursdays. They didn't all come each time, but there was always at least one and usually as many as four or five. My house was turning into some kind of brainiac high school hangout.

It was only a matter of time before that caused trouble.

CHAPTER 18

ANYBODY who's grown up in Colorado can tell you that there's one day of the year when we're guaranteed to have bad weather: Halloween. It looked like this year would be no exception. It was damp outside and had just dropped below freezing when Brian called me the evening of October thirtieth.

"Jared!" He sounded frantic. "Lizzy's water broke. Get to the hospital! *Now!*"

Once I found my way to the maternity section, I paced outside the door of her room for a few minutes. I wasn't sure if I should knock or just go in. I didn't know if things were just starting, or if she was actually pushing. Would she have her feet up in stirrups? Would there be blood everywhere? I had exactly zero experience with childbirth and had no idea what to expect.

I eventually caught one of the nurses as she went into the room and asked her to tell Brian that I was waiting outside. It must have been all of half a second later when he came flying out of the room.

"What the hell are you doing out here? Get in there!" He was obviously freaking out. I had never seen him look so frazzled. His hair was sticking every which way, and his eyes were huge.

"Has she had the baby?"

"No! But she's going to start pushing soon, and she wants you in there!"

"What?" I was having horrific mental images of Lizzy in stirrups, parts of her body neither of us wanted me to see, and lots of blood. "No! I can't be in there while she's having the baby!"

Brian grabbed the front of my shirt and got in my face like he hadn't done since we were both teenagers. He was really shaken up. "Lizzy wants you in there. And if that's what she wants, then that's what she gets, even if I have to kick your ass and drag you in there by the hair to get it! *Understand*?"

"Okay! Brian, settle down. I'm coming."

So Brian stood on one side and I stood on the other, holding Lizzy's hand while she pushed. It went on for more than an hour, and poor Lizzy was a mess by the end. I had never been so happy to be male.

Finally, the doctor stuck something on the baby's head that looked suspiciously like a funnel. Lizzy gave one last push, the doctor pulled, and the baby was free. A boy. He was bald and pink and wrinkly, his head was shaped like the funnel, and he had an angry red triangle right above the bridge of his nose. I was horrified, but Lizzy assured me all of that would pass.

"We're naming him James Henry," she told me proudly. James, my middle name, and Henry, my dad's name. I kissed her on the forehead.

Brian brought him over and started to pass him to me.

"What are you doing? I can't hold him! What if I hurt him?"

He laughed at me. "Better get used to it, little brother. Lizzy told me about the weekly date nights you promised us."

"You mean the weekly date nights she coerced me into?"

But once he was in my arms, I saw that he really was beautiful.

And precious. And the horrible tightness that had held my heart since Matt left eased just a tiny bit.

I laughed out loud. "I'm an uncle!"

THE first Tuesday in November, seven different kids were around my dining room table when there was a knock on the door. Matt was the only person who didn't ring the doorbell, and I tried to beat back the ridiculous excitement that he was here.

But when I opened my door, it was immediately apparent that this was not a social visit. It was Matt, in full uniform, and another cop was with him. Matt was obviously extremely embarrassed. He had his hat off and was fidgeting with it. He was looking everywhere but at me. I was trying desperately not to think about the way his lips felt on my neck, his hands in my hair, his body pressing against mine—

"Sir?" It was the other cop talking, interrupting my treacherous thoughts, and I found it difficult to tear my eyes away from Matt and look at him. "We got a call that you have some kids here?"

It took me a second to process his words. "Yes." I stepped aside so they could see the kids at the table. It seemed obvious to me what was going on: a bunch of kids, two pizza boxes, and at least a dozen open school books. The kids were all frozen, staring at the door, with pencils and floppy pieces of pizza in their hands. It looked like some crazy parody of *The Last Supper*. The cop—his tag said Officer Jameson—stalked past me to the table.

"What's going on here? Which one of you is Aiden?"

Aiden turned about ten shades of red and raised his hand.

"Is this everybody?" Jameson asked. "Are there any kids back in the bedroom?"

"*What?*" I almost yelled, and at the same time, I heard Matt say, "Grant, don't!" Grant just smirked at him.

The implications of what was going on were starting to catch up with me. I took a deep breath and said, "No, there's nobody in the bedroom! How can you even ask that? I'm tutoring them."

Jameson was opening his mouth to say something, and I could tell it was going to be something sarcastic, when Matt jumped in.

"Jared." I could tell by his face that he hated saying it. "We got a call from one of the moms." I heard Aiden groan. "She was worried about her kid spending so much time here. She asked us to check it out."

"I'm not doing anything wrong." My jaw was clenched so tight, I was surprised they could understand me.

Officer Grant Jameson snorted.

Matt shot him a dirty look but said to me, "I know." He looked at the floor, fidgeted more with his hat. "She was pretty upset, and she's been making calls to some of the other parents. I'm sorry." Now he looked back up at me, and I hated myself for the way my heart skipped a beat, just looking into his eyes. "I think it might be best if you had them go home."

"This is bullshit!" Ringo suddenly yelled, standing up from the table. "Jared is the only one who's been able to teach us this stuff. You can't make us leave."

Jameson turned on him. "Look, kid—"

"Stop!" Amazingly, he did, and everybody looked at me. I turned to Jameson. "This is my house, and you have no right to come in here like this. I'm not doing anything wrong, and I would like you to leave. Right now." I looked at Matt and said, "Both of you!" Matt flinched and looked away.

Jameson opened his mouth to speak, but I wasn't done. I turned to the students. "I certainly don't want anybody thinking I'm

107

corrupting their kids." I tried not to sound too sarcastic when I said that. "I think the officer is right. You should all go home."

This was met by loud protests, mainly voiced in the form of obscenities, from the kids.

"Jared, you can't quit teaching us now. We need your help," Ringo said. "Since you started helping us, we're all passing."

One of the other boys jumped in. "Right. This is the first year that I've been able to keep playing football. Every other year, my math grades are too low for eligibility."

"Listen, I'll keep teaching—"

"Sir, I don't think—"Jameson tried to cut in, but I just raised my voice and talked over him.

"—but anybody who comes back, you need to bring a note from your parents saying that it's okay. Tell the others too. And I know your handwriting, so don't try to forge it."

Everybody looked relieved at that except Aiden. There didn't seem to be much I could do about that, though.

The kids finally left, and Jameson headed for the car, but Matt hung back.

He was watching me warily. I was gathering up dirty paper plates and empty pop cans, doing my best not to look at him. "Jared, I'm sorry. I know you wouldn't do anything inappropriate." I didn't say anything. Whatever anger I had started with was gone, and I just felt embarrassed and resentful. "This is why, isn't it?" he asked quietly. "This is why you aren't teaching? It's not really about the shop at all."

"Yes." And I hated how defeated I sounded when I said it.

"Maybe you could—"

I didn't want to talk to him about it. Not now, with everything else lying unfinished between us. I looked up at him and said, with more venom than I felt, "Will that be all, Officer Richards?" I could tell I had hurt him, but I didn't care. He looked away.

"That's all."

I resisted the urge to slam the door behind him.

CHAPTER 19

ON THURSDAY, most of my students came back with permission slips. A few of the parents had actually written encouraging notes, telling me that they trusted me and that they appreciated what I was doing for their kids. It made me feel better, and after that the tutoring sessions resumed without incident.

A few days later, Cole called.

"Hey, Sweets. Are you lonely tonight?" He always talked in a flirty, flamboyant, lilting voice, and he never called me by name.

"We'll both be lonely tonight if you call me that again." I knew he wouldn't listen.

"Don't be such a kill-joy."

"Are you in Vail? The slopes aren't even open yet, are they?"

"Just passing through, Sweets. I thought I could head your way for the night. That is, if you're feeling accommodating."

My first instinct was to say no. But who was I kidding? I knew Matt wasn't celibate in his relationship with Cherie, and I certainly didn't owe him anything on that front. Plus, I don't get that many opportunities. There was no telling when Cole would call again— maybe as soon as next month, maybe not until next year. Maybe never. And the thought of the months stretching out ahead of me with no company but my own hand decided it for me.

"Cole, your timing could not be better."

"I'll be there in four hours, Sweets."

The next morning, when I came out of the bedroom, he was already dressed. Cole is shorter than me, whip thin, boyishly cute with dark hair artfully cut to hang in his eyes, and has just a hint of swish in his walk. He was looking at me oddly out of the corner his eye.

"What?"

"Just wondering, Sweets, that's all. Who exactly is Matt?"

I felt myself go red up to my hairline and thought back on our activities of the previous night, hoping I hadn't said Matt's name at an inopportune moment. Cole must have seen the slight panic on my face because he laughed.

"Not that. I've told you before—you talk in your sleep." He turned and pinned me with a piercing gaze. "Are you in a relationship? I know things between us have always been casual, but I would expect better of you than to cheat on a lover."

"No. It's not like that at all." I tried to sound nonchalant but failed. Instead, it came out resigned and bitter.

He relaxed. "But you want it to be?" There was no jealousy. Our relationship was casual enough to avoid that kind of snag. He was just asking.

"I do."

"So what's the problem? He's not interested?"

"Let's just say his closet door is shut tight. And deadbolted."

"Ah. The power of denial. Well, then, I don't feel bad about last night. Do you?"

I smiled at him and leaned in to kiss his jaw. "Not a bit." It was mostly true. "I probably should take you out for breakfast."

"You should, but you won't. I know you. God forbid anybody in this town find out that you actually get laid once in a while."

It was an old argument and one that we never pursued far. "Cole—"

"Don't worry. I'll wait here while you run to the store and get something. And don't even think about bringing me a donut. I want a—"

"A cinnamon bagel with low-fat cream cheese and a vanilla latte. I know." I kissed him again. "Just give me five minutes to shower first."

Just as I was stepping out of the shower, I heard a knock on the door, and my heart sank. I knew it was Matt—anybody else would use the doorbell—and I was struggling to get my sweats back on and get out there, although I had no idea how I was going to handle the situation when I did.

I heard the door open and heard Cole say, "Well, *hello*, officer! If I had known we had company coming, I wouldn't have gotten dressed so fast." Oh shit.

I made it into the living room, pants on but with my hair dripping wet, just in time to hear Matt say, "So. You must be Cole."

"Well." Cole threw a wink over his shoulder at me. "I'm flattered. And you are…?"

Matt just stood there. He was in his uniform, and I had never seen him look so angry. He was looking at Cole like he was some kind of bug and he couldn't decide whether to put him outside or just step on him. But Cole is not the type to be intimidated. If anything, he uses his flamboyance as a type of shield, a way to thumb his nose at people who look down on him. I watched him do it now. He put his hand on his hip, cocked it out a bit, looked flirtingly up at Matt through his bangs, and even batted his eyes a little. "Is there a problem, officer?"

Matt's cheeks started to flush, but I didn't know if it was embarrassment or anger. He was completely still and silent. When it became obvious that he wasn't going to answer Cole, I spoke up.

"Cole, this is Matt."

Cole's eyes went a little wide, and then he was instantly in motion. "Okay, Sweets, it's *obviously* time for me to be on my way. Give me one second." Matt and I stood there, arms crossed, watching each other warily while Cole bustled around gathering up his jacket and keys. Then he stepped up next to me and put an arm around my waist. He leaned in to nuzzle my neck, and I tilted my head a little to give him better access. Matt went stone cold rigid. I was still mad enough over the tutoring incident to take a little bit of pleasure in making him uncomfortable.

"An absolute *pleasure*, as always, Sweets. I'll give you a call next time I'm in the area." He intentionally said it loud enough for Matt to hear but then whispered in my ear, "Go get him, Jared," before kissing me on the cheek and heading for the door.

Matt and I stood there a little longer after he was gone, waiting to see who would speak first. It turned out to be him.

"I didn't expect you to have company."

"Obviously." All those weeks that I had been hoping to see him, hoping he would call, hoping he would knock on my door just like he had this morning, and yet now that he was here, all I could see was the judgment in his eyes. I turned away from him, went around the counter into the kitchen, and started making coffee.

"What is it, Matt? Did you come here to talk or to tell me how disgusted you are by my lifestyle? Or maybe to make sure I'm not tutoring kids in my *bedroom*?"

"Not that. I wanted to see you. But, I didn't expect—" He stopped and seemed to be struggling to find the right words, struggling to get his rage back under control. "I didn't expect *him*. I didn't expect to find you with somebody else!"

"Why not, Matt? Why shouldn't I be with somebody else?"

"Do you love him?"

That surprised me, but I didn't answer him. Instead I asked, "Do you love Cherie?"

"No."

A flat, honest answer. I was trying to hang on to my anger, because I knew if it left, I would only feel dirty and depressed. "No. I don't love Cole. You know that." I looked over at him. "If I had things my way, it would have been you in my bed last night. Last night and every night. But you have made it quite clear that you want nothing to do with me."

He was staring at the wall about a foot above my head, and I knew he was struggling. He was angry and hurt and embarrassed, and I was pretty sure he was at least a little bit jealous too.

"I love only you. But if you expect me to apologize for going on with my life after *you* walked out of it without a backward glance, you can go to hell."

He stood there another minute, still not looking at me. Finally, he said, "I think I should go."

"I think you should too."

THE next evening, he was back. I heard him knock, and when I opened door, he was there. He was leaning against the doorframe with a six pack in one hand. He looked haggard, and embarrassed, and scared to death.

"You look like hell."

A hint of smile flickered on his face and was gone.

"Are you alone?" I was glad to hear that there was no judgment in his voice. He was simply trying to let me establish a boundary if I wanted to.

"I am."

He sighed and then said softly, "Can we try this again, please? Last time didn't really go the way I planned."

And any anger or resentment I still had over those last unfortunate visits vanished. I was just glad he had come back. "Of course."

"I heard about the baby," he told me as he came in. "I guess you're Uncle Jarhead now?"

I laughed, probably louder than I should have.

He went in the kitchen to put the beer away, came back out with two open ones and handed one to me. And then there was a moment when we both just stood there.

For my part, I couldn't get enough of looking at him, and it was all I could do not to throw my arms around him and hug him. It wasn't a romantic urge. Sure, I was crazy about him, but we hadn't been lovers. We had been friends. And it was losing *that* which had hurt the most. Just having him walk back through my door—without the thunder clouds raging in his eyes, like last time—made me feel like I could breathe for the first time in weeks.

For his part, he still looked scared out of his wits, and he was looking everywhere but at me. I think he was waiting for me to say something or to yell at him, but he finally glanced at me, and I was still just standing there grinning at him like a damn fool. His eyebrows went up a little in surprise, and I managed to say, "It's really good to see you."

He looked relieved and clapped me on the back so hard that I staggered a little bit. "Let's go sit down."

So we sat down in our usual spots, side by side on the couch like we had a million times before. It felt so familiar. He leaned back with a sigh and sat there with his head back and his eyes closed. I could tell he was still wound up tight, but I could also see that he was glad to be here.

"So how did you hear about the baby?"

He sat up and started fidgeting with the label on his beer bottle—another gesture that was achingly familiar. "Cherie told me."

I felt jealousy, hot and angry in my chest, and tried to force it down. But my voice was sharper than I intended when I asked, "How is Cherie?"

"How is she?" He made an angry laugh. "Christ, Jared, she's awful. She's boring. She wears too much perfume. She hates being outside and hates the mountains. She babbles through the football games. She doesn't even know what a first down is. And she only talks about two things: how much she hates her job and how much she hates her piece of shit ex-husband."

"Um...." I was fighting to keep the smile off of my face.

He was quiet for a minute but then said, "The worst part is I knew all of that going into it." He glanced over at me. "Aren't you going to tell me what a fucking idiot I am?"

"Would that make you feel better?"

He laughed without much humor and went back to picking at the label. "These last few weeks have been miserable."

That hit me. I was quiet for a minute, but then I managed to say quietly, "They've been miserable for me too."

"I've missed you." It was barely a whisper. But when I started to reach across to him, he said, "Don't."

I pulled back, feeling stricken.

116

"I didn't mean it like that." He sighed and leaned back again. "I just... I'm not ready for that yet. I just need—" He stopped, bit his lower lip, and stared at the ceiling. "I know I have no right to ask you for anything, but can I just stay here for a bit? I just...." He took a shaking breath, "I just want to be *here*. Please?"

"Anything."

So I turned on the TV, and we nursed our beers. We mostly talked football and easily fell back into our old banter—a little more awkward than before, but it still felt great. And I watched him slowly relax, layers of tension and sadness falling away, and he even smiled once, if only for a second. Eventually, he leaned back, and within minutes, he was asleep.

When I got up in the morning, he was gone.

THE next day, Ringo came into the back of the shop to get me.

"Jared, Mrs. Rochester is here to see you." I knew by his voice he was concerned about it.

It took me a minute to place the name. "You mean, Alice Rochester?"

"I don't know her first name."

"The high school principal?"

"Yes."

"Shit." After the incident with the police, all but two of my students had returned with permission slips. But it seemed that wasn't enough. Some parent had obviously called the school to complain. "Tell her I'll be right out." And then I spent a few seconds composing myself, getting ready for what I was sure was going to be an ugly confrontation.

117

Mrs. Rochester was in her forties. She was in good shape and had on a navy blue skirt and matching jacket. "Mr. Thomas!" She was smiling when she shook my hand. She had teeth so white and perfect she could have been in toothpaste commercials. "I don't think we've ever officially met before."

"Call me Jared."

"Jared. You can call me Alice." She was still smiling. "You may not realize what a buzz you've created at our school."

I was annoyed at her cheerfulness but said, "I'm really sorry about that. I was just trying to help."

She looked a little confused. "Why are you sorry?"

"You're talking about the tutoring, right?"

"Of course. I know this is unexpected, but I wanted to ask you if you would be willing to meet with me and a couple of the teachers, just for a few minutes?"

"Shit." Had I said that out loud?

"Excuse me?"

"Nothing." I took a deep breath and made an effort to smile. "I'm sorry. Yes, I'll come if you think it's important."

"Oh good," she said with obvious relief. The toothpaste smile was back. "This close to Thanksgiving is crazy for everybody. How about the first Monday in December? Could you come to the school at three thirty?"

"Sure."

When she was gone, Ringo asked, "What was that all about?"

"*That* was probably the end of our tutoring sessions."

CHAPTER 20

TWO nights later, Matt was pounding on my front door hard enough to rattle the hinges.

"I broke up with Cherie," he said as soon as he walked in.

"Oh." I hoped the joy those words awoke in me wasn't too evident in my voice. "Why?"

He glanced sideways at me, and there was anger in his eyes.

"Don't! Don't do that. You know why."

"Matt—"

"*No!*"

I went silent, my heart in my throat. He was pacing back and forth, looking angrier with every pass. I was pretty sure anything I said would be the wrong thing, so I just waited. Suddenly he turned and drove his fist into the wall.

"Feel better now?" I asked.

"No." He leaned against the wall with his head in his hands. There was blood on the paint, and the drywall was going to need to be patched.

Finally he spoke. "I feel like I haven't slept in weeks." It sounded like he might break into tears at any moment. "I'm so

119

fucking tired. And I'm so confused. Part of me wants to kiss you, and part of me wants to just beat the hell out of you."

I have to admit I was a little bit alarmed by that. "Do I get a vote? Because I definitely prefer one over the other." He didn't laugh.

"I wish I could stop thinking about you. I wish I didn't miss you so much."

"I miss you, too, Matt," I said honestly. "I'd give anything for us to just be friends again."

He didn't answer for a moment but then said without looking at me, "You could be happy with just being friends?"

"It wouldn't be my first choice, but yes, if that's what you want." It was the truth. Better that than to be alone again.

Another short silence, and then, quietly, he said, "I don't know if I can do it, Jared. I wish I could. But I don't think I can go back to that." He took a deep, shaking breath and finally looked at me. "I miss you so much, but I wish I didn't want you the way I do."

"Why do you have to fight it, Matt? Why can't you just accept that you're as attracted to me as I am to you?" It was the wrong thing to say.

He grabbed my arms and slammed me against the wall. "You think it's so easy! I've spent my whole life denying these feelings. I don't know if I can accept them now. I don't know if I *want* to accept them!" His face was only a foot away from mine. The look in his eyes was torture. It was pain, and fear, and loathing, and desire, all fighting for dominance. I couldn't look at him. I couldn't bear to see it.

But when I dropped my gaze, I stopped short. In looking down, away from his face, my gaze had inadvertently landed on his crotch. And I was surprised to see that he was fully erect. I could see the telling bulge inside his jeans. Knowing I was possibly making a huge mistake, hands shaking in both fear and anticipation, I reached out—he still had my arms pinned to the wall, and I could barely reach—and started to unbutton his pants.

He went completely still. I don't think he was even breathing. Then, "What are you doing?" I didn't look at his face. His hands were still on my biceps. He could easily stop me if he chose to.

"Taking a chance." My hands were shaking a little less now, but I was waiting for him to step away, to yell, maybe even to punch me. The last buttons came undone and his erection, covered in the smooth black of his briefs, was pushing through the flaps of denim.

"I don't think you should be doing that." But his voice had gone low and husky.

"I'm sure you're right," I replied, and I brushed my fingertips lightly over the fabric that still covered him. His breath caught in his throat, but he didn't move. I flattened my hand against him, felt the whole length of him against my palm, and squeezed a little. He gasped a little, then gave a small sigh of surrender, and took a last tiny step towards me, his forehead hitting the wall above my shoulder. His hands slid down from my arms to rest on my waistband. I rubbed him harder, pushing my fingers down inside of his jeans. I could tell by his breathing that he was becoming more aroused. Was he even leaning into my hand, or was that my imagination? I didn't want to push him too far, and yet, maybe....

I stopped, wondering what exactly I was expecting. And then, barely a whisper, I heard in my ear: "Jared, please don't stop."

I didn't hesitate. With one hand, I pulled the waistband of his briefs down out of the way. When my right hand closed around him, he groaned low in his throat. I started to stroke him, softly at first but then harder as his breathing quickened. His fingers were gripping my sides so hard I was sure I would have bruises. His head was resting against the wall next to mine, his face in my hair. Soft lips and sandpaper stubble both brushed my skin. He wasn't kissing me. He wasn't even moving, but I could feel his breath hot against

121

my neck, and it felt wonderful.

I grabbed his shirt with my free hand, turned, and pushed him against the wall. I dropped to my knees in front of him and took him into my mouth, as deep as I could. He actually stopped breathing, held his breath for a few seconds, and I thought he was going to stop me. But then it all came out in a low moan, and he relaxed against the wall behind him.

I had my hand around the base of his cock, and I worked my mouth up and down, trailing my tongue in a circle around his head every time I reached the top. I couldn't remember ever being more turned on in my life. I was dying to kiss him and pull all his clothes off him and fuck him—or have him fuck me, I didn't care which. But he certainly wasn't ready for that yet. So I just kept sucking and licking and pumping a little on the bottom of his shaft with my fist. He was definitely responding, pushing into me and moaning. I noticed that his hands kept reaching for me, but then he would pull them back and clench them at his sides again. Finally one landed on my shoulder and touched my hair a little. I remembered my birthday, the way he had held me against the counter with both of his hands in my hair, and I knew what he wanted.

I stopped just long enough to say, "You can grab. Just don't push," before returning to sucking him.

He actually gasped out, "Oh Jesus, thank you," and his hands both gripped tight into my hair. He didn't push. Actually, he didn't have time. As soon as he grabbed me like that, he groaned, and he started to come. Despite being caught off guard, I managed to swallow fast without choking and kept sucking until the tremors had stopped.

Only then did it occur to me that I didn't really know where to go from here. My own erection was begging for some attention, and I tried to talk it down. What had happened felt less like sex and more like stress release, like letting steam out of a pressure cooker. I knew I couldn't expect any kind of return.

His fingers pulled out of my hair, but before I could stand up, he slid down the wall to sit in front of me with his face buried in his hands. He leaned into me, just barely. I started to put my arms around him, but that made him tense up immediately, so I settled for one on his shoulder, the other on the back of his neck.

I felt like I had to say something, but had no idea what. "Matt?" And then I heard his breath catch again. Not like before. A torn, shuddering breath—and I realized he was crying.

"Hey, it's okay," I whispered. Whatever I had been expecting, it wasn't this.

"I'm so ashamed." His voice was so quiet I could barely hear him.

My heart fell a little. My intention had certainly not been to shame him in any way. "Look, I'm sorry—"

"No." He took a deep breath and then said in a rush, "I'm ashamed of how much I liked it. How good it felt. How much I wanted it. How I want it to happen again already. Nothing, with any girl, has ever felt as good as that. It was...." His arms slid around my waist and held me tight. "Oh God, Jared...." The despair in his voice was enough to break my heart. But there was something else in his voice too. Something that sounded like awe.

"We don't need to talk about that right now. You're exhausted. I shouldn't have pushed you like that. I think what you really need is some sleep. What do you think?"

I was talking to him like I might talk to a scared child, but it seemed to work. He took another deep, shaking breath, let go of me, and stood up, turning away from me while he got his pants back in place. He wouldn't look at me, but there was no anger in his face, only sadness and confusion ... and just maybe relief. "Yeah, I think I could sleep now." But he wasn't moving.

I stood up too and gently turned him around and pushed him toward the bedroom. He went, but then he stood there looking at the bed with something like terror in his eyes.

"Take the bed," I said gently. "I'll sleep on the couch tonight."

I tried not to feel hurt at how relieved he looked. He stripped down to his shorts and climbed into the bed. Once again, I felt like I should say something, but I had no idea what he needed to hear right now. That I loved him? That my heart was breaking for the pain he was in? That I was sorry for pushing him, or that I wanted nothing more than to climb in beside him and make love to him all night? What I settled for was, "Well, goodnight."

I was at the door headed for the couch when I heard him quietly say my name. "Jared? Will you lay here with me? I don't want you to go." He was facing away from me, still not able to turn around and look at me.

"I'll do anything you need me to do. But...." I hesitated. "Are you sure that's what you want?" I hardly dared to hope.

"I'm sure. Just lay here with me. Nothing else. I really just want you close. That's all."

"Of course." That did leave me with a quandary of what to do about my clothes. To undress first felt like it would be adding a level of pressure I was sure he didn't need right now. On the other hand, I didn't really want to sleep fully clothed. I stood there for a second, telling myself I was a fool for worrying about it. I finally pulled off my shoes and socks and T-shirt but decided to keep my pants on and climbed in beside him. I lay facing his back. We would have been spooning except for the foot of empty space between us. He sighed. Even from where I was, a foot away, I could feel some of the tension leaving him.

"Just a little closer, okay? I want... I just want to know you're here."

I moved a little closer, so that I was almost against his back, our skin barely touching. My own body was responding to the nearness of his smooth back. I made sure that part of me wasn't against him. He didn't need that right now. I put one arm over him. "Sleep now, okay? We can worry about everything else later."

His breathing was already slowing down, and I thought he might already be asleep when he said quietly, "Thank you."

What I thought was, *I hope you still feel that way in the morning.* What I said was, "Anytime." And then he was asleep. I was awake for a long time after that, wondering what was going to happen when he woke up. Then, in his sleep, he shifted closer, leaning back against me, and made a contented sigh that made my heart break all over again. I wrapped my arm tightly around him and told myself to take my own advice. We could worry about everything else later.

I AWOKE once in the night and got up long enough to use the john, brush my teeth, and take off my damn jeans. When I got back into bed, he immediately moved back into my arms, although he didn't say a word. When I woke in the morning, I was surprised to see that he was still there. He was normally such an early riser that I had fully expected him to be gone by the time I woke up. The slight tension in his back and the sound of his breathing told me that he was awake. He had to be able to feel my morning erection pressing against his back side, but he didn't move away.

"You were talking again."

I laughed. "What did I say this time?"

He hesitated for a minute and then said quietly, "You said my name."

Still he hadn't moved. I asked, "How do you feel?"

A deep sigh, and then: "A lot better."

"And how do you feel about this?" I tightened my arm around

him a little to let him know what I meant.

And I knew he was smiling although his voice was very quiet when he said, "A lot better."

My heart skipped a beat. "Really?"

"I've been awake for a while, thinking. And I realized a few things." He stopped for a moment, and I waited. "I dated quite a few girls over the years. I was attracted to them, and I even cared about a couple of them. But I never loved any of them. And the relationships just weren't ever very satisfying. They always seemed like more trouble than they were worth. And so I gave up. I decided that I just wasn't really cut out for it, that I liked being a bachelor, and that I wasn't ever dating again. And actually, my life got a lot easier after that.

"And sometimes I would be physically attracted to other men. But it wasn't ever anybody I really *knew*, so I ignored it. I didn't want those feelings, and I buried them down deep inside of me until they were gone.

"And things were okay for a while. But you know how it is. Pretty soon, all of my friends were married. And I always felt like a fifth wheel." Yes, I did know how that felt. "The only time I wasn't the odd man out was when they were trying to hook me up with someone, and that was worse. So I started making excuses, quit hanging out with them. And one day I woke up and realized that they were gone.

"So I changed jobs, and I moved here. And I met you. I was so tired of being lonely, and I was so glad to finally find somebody to just hang out with."

I squeezed him when he said that and whispered, "Me too."

"All summer, we had so much fun together, and I was so happy to have you. And that happiness just kept growing. It got bigger and bigger until it was all I thought about. Every day when I woke up, I couldn't wait to see you again. It was such a great feeling. And I guess I'm an idiot, because I truly didn't recognize what it meant." He stopped, but I knew he wasn't done. "And that would have been okay, too, except then, just out of the fucking blue, there were the, well, the *urges* that went with those feelings. *Strong* urges. And that was something I honestly had not expected at all. They caught me completely off guard. Well, I don't think I need to tell you, it freaked me right the fuck out."

"Yeah, I noticed." But I said it teasingly. "And how about now? Does it still freak you out?"

"A little. Not as much. I've had a lot of time to think about it the past few weeks. It's been hard for me to get used to the idea of being with another man, but...." He stopped for a second, and I could hear a smile in his voice when he went on, "I think last night helped quite a bit."

I smiled too. "I'm glad I took that chance, then."

"Me too." I could tell by his voice that he was blushing. "But I don't mean just that. I woke up a couple of hours ago, and my first thought was that I should leave before you woke up. But I realized I didn't want to leave. I realized...." He paused for second, took a deep breath, and said, "I really like being here."

"You're always welcome at my house. You know that."

"No. I mean"—and I felt his hand on my arm, where it was wrapped around him—"I like being *here*."

"Oh." *Here* in my bed. In my arms. Was that really what he was telling me? My heart was suddenly racing. Once I thought I could keep my voice level, I asked, as casually as I could, trying to hide the insane hope that was suddenly flooding through me, "Are you saying that you want to be with me?"

A pause, and then, his voice full of amazement, he said, "I think maybe I want to try."

I held him tighter, my forehead against the nape of his neck,

127

and tried to just concentrate on breathing for a minute. I felt him there against me, so big and strong and yet so vulnerable. Could this really be happening? I wanted to cry. I wanted to tell him I loved him. I wanted so much to kiss him, to touch him everywhere, to shed what little clothing was between us, to spend the whole day in bed with him. But I also knew this was a big step for him, and I didn't want to push him. My erection, which had gone down as we had been talking, was suddenly back, and I didn't know if I should be trying to hide that fact from him or not.

"Jared, say something."

My voice was shaking. "Like what?"

"What do you want?"

"Matt." I tightened my arms around him, kissed his neck, and slid one hand up his smooth stomach to his chest. "All I've ever wanted is you."

He sighed and relaxed into my arms. I kissed his neck some more and let my hand explore his chest and then his stomach. My fingers found that amazing trail of hair leading down from his navel and started to follow it. He moaned a little as my fingers moved lower. I reached down and put my hand over the bulge in his briefs, felt his erection jump against my hand. And suddenly, before I even knew it, he had jumped out of bed like he was spring loaded and started putting his pants on.

"Shit. Matt, I'm sorry…."

"Don't be sorry." His cheeks were red with embarrassment, but he looked right at me, so I knew he meant what he said. "You don't need to be sorry. Just… not yet, okay?"

The words "not yet" sounded so much like a promise that my heart swelled. "Okay."

"I'll make coffee. You can have the shower first."

There was a cup of coffee waiting for me on the counter when

I emerged from the shower. He was staring into the fridge with a frown on his face.

"Why do you have so much mustard, anyway?"

"It's Eddy Mac mustard."

"What?"

"You know—Ed McCaffrey. He used to play for the Broncos. He makes mustard now, and the money goes to some charity. I was trying to do my part."

He gave me the pseudo-grin. "You're such a philanthropist." He closed the fridge. "Seriously, what do you have to eat? I'm starving."

"There are some Pop-Tarts in the cabinet. And some Fruit Loops. Although I wouldn't use the milk if I were you. And I have some peanut butter, but I'm out of bread."

He leaned on the counter, looked in my eyes, and said, "We'll definitely need to do something about this kitchen. Are you working today?"

"Yes. I get off at five."

"Do you have an extra house key?"

"Yes."

"Can I have it?"

"Of course."

"I need to go home and change, and then I'll do some shopping and meet you here after work."

And that sounded a little bit like a promise too.

CHAPTER 21

WHEN I got home, he was in the kitchen putting water on the stove to cook spaghetti in.

"Here." He tossed me a yellow bell pepper. "Cut that up for the salad, will you? I got an avocado for you too." He hated avocados.

"What are *you* gonna do?"

He winked at me. "Supervise, of course." He leaned against the counter next to me, and I started chopping. "I've been meaning to ask how the tutoring is going."

I told him about Ringo and about the visit from Alice Rochester. I don't cook, so it took me a ridiculously long time to cut up the pepper and avocado. I noticed he was moving closer as I talked, but I kept my eyes on the cutting board in front of me.

Then I felt that gentle tug on the back of my head, and it felt like my heart stopped beating. Such a tiny, innocent thing as he pulled gently on my curls, but it hit me all at once that he really had come back to me. I realized I had stopped talking, stopped moving; maybe I had even stopped breathing. I almost wanted to cry but fought it. I made myself take a breath and found that I was shaking.

"What's wrong?" he whispered, almost in my ear.

"I missed this," I said quietly.

"I missed you." He stepped closer. "Jared, I want to try something. Like an experiment. Is that okay?"

"Last time you asked a question like that, it ended with you not speaking to me for almost two months." I tried to say it lightly, but I didn't quite pull it off.

He lightly wrapped his arms around me and put his face in my hair. "I know. I'm sorry."

I thought about it for a minute. I had an idea what he had in mind. "I don't want to be alone anymore. Whatever you want this to be between us, I can handle it. Just don't leave me again."

"Never. I promise. I learned my lesson."

I took a deep breath, tried to slow my speeding heart, and turned to face him. "Okay."

He pulled me close, then took my face in his hands, and looked into my eyes. I started to put my arms around him, but he tensed up and said, "No. Don't do that."

"I'm not allowed to touch you?"

"Not yet."

"What do you want me to do then?"

"Stop talking." He was so serious I might have laughed if my heart wasn't pounding so hard. I closed my eyes and tried to relax.

He was combing his fingers through my hair, and I remembered my birthday—his hands in my hair and his weight against me, his lips against my neck, and then him walking out the door.

"Relax, Jared," he whispered, and I pulled my mind away from that night. It would not end like that. Whatever happened, he had promised not to leave again. I felt him lean in. Felt his breath against my lips and then the faintest brush of his lips over my mouth— soft, warm lips against mine. It was all I could do to keep my hands at my side. Then he actually kissed me, firm but gentle, his lips just barely parted.

He never said I couldn't kiss back.

I opened my mouth, leaned into him, and brushed the tip of my tongue against his lips.

Whatever wall he had been trying to keep between us crumbled away at that slight touch. He moaned, and suddenly he was *really* kissing me, his arms tight around me, his tongue touching mine, his body pressing hard against me. This time, he didn't object when I put my arms around him.

An eternity later, he pulled back a little. One hand was in my hair, his other arm around my waist, and his forehead was against mine.

"Was that the result you were expecting?" I asked breathlessly.

He closed his eyes but didn't pull away. He took a deep breath and just barely shook his head. "No."

"You didn't think you would like it."

This time, a slight nod. "At the very least, I thought it would be like some of the women I've kissed: pleasant but uninspiring."

That made me smile. "And instead...?"

"Oh God." His breath was shaky. He looked into my eyes and smiled back. "*Very* inspiring."

I pulled him to me and kissed him again, and his response was fierce and urgent. It felt almost like an attack that I couldn't quite fend off. His tongue was pushing into my mouth. He had a handful of my hair, gripped so tight that I couldn't move my head without hurting myself. The counter behind me was digging painfully into my back side. I put my hands under his shirt, started to feel the hard muscles on his chest. He stopped kissing me just long enough to pull his shirt off, and to my surprise, he pulled mine off as well. Then his arms were back around me, one hand back in my hair, his mouth warm and insistent against mine. His skin was smooth and seemed feverishly hot. He felt amazing. His body was so strong and solid and perfect under my hands. I couldn't remember the last time a kiss had felt so passionate and arousing.

His hands were fumbling at the buttons on my jeans. He tore them open and shoved one hand down the front of my pants. His grip was hard and rough, not quite painful, and I wanted more of it. I was gasping, arching against him, hoping I wouldn't embarrass myself by coming before we even got our clothes off.

"Jesus, Jared." His voice in my ear sounded a little frantic. "I don't really know what to do."

I laughed a little at that. I should have realized I would need to take the lead.

I unbuttoned his pants and slid them down just far enough to free his erection. He followed my lead and did the same to me. He was taller than me, so I wrapped one arm around his neck, pulled myself up a little while pulling him down, until our cocks were even, then wrapped my hand around both of them and started to stroke us off together.

The look on his face might have made me laugh, any other time. He looked so surprised as he looked down at my hand pumping away on both of us. He looked up into my eyes and said breathlessly, "I wouldn't have thought of that."

I really did laugh then.

But then his hand stopped mine. "I want to do it."

Not like I was going to argue. I wrapped my other arm around his neck, which allowed me to hold myself up at his height a little easier, propped against the counter. I kissed him again and felt his big, strong hand start to work. I really wished we had our pants off, that we were somewhere other than in the kitchen with the counter

133

digging into me from behind, but there was no way I was going to stop him now. He was moaning into my mouth, and his fist was moving faster, and—

His phone rang.

The whole world stopped.

"Shit!" he whispered, without pulling his mouth from mine.

"Matt." His hand was still in the same place, although it had stopped moving. "Please tell me you're not going to answer that."

It rang again. He had left it on the coffee table in the living room. Technically, it was the property of the Coda Police Department. I had only seen him use it a couple of times.

"I have to." His head was on my shoulder, and he was breathing hard. We both were. "You're the only person besides the department who has that number. And since it's obviously not you calling...." Another ring. "Shit!" He took a deep, shuddering breath and pushed his face into my hair for just a second, and then he seemed to tear himself away from me.

He was in the living room, on the phone. I wasn't listening. I was mostly trying to get my breathing back under control, pulling my pants back up but hoping they weren't going to stay there for long. But when he came back a minute later, I knew something was wrong. He was deathly white, and his hands were shaking a little as he put his shirt back on and started searching for his keys.

"Matt, what's wrong?"

"Cherie's dead." There was no emotion in his voice when he said it. He sounded like it was just business, but I could tell by the tension in his shoulders and around his eyes that he was upset.

"*What?*"

"She was murdered. Somebody shot her last night. I have to go."

I was stunned. People aren't murdered in Coda. People die, of course. We had our share of teenagers killed in drunk-driving accidents or middle-aged men killed in hunting mishaps. But murder? That didn't happen.

"But... how?"

"Jared, I don't know. I don't know much. I have to go in for questioning."

"*What?*"

I couldn't believe how calm he was. "As far as any of them know, I'm her boyfriend. Remember? Even if they knew I had broken it off, which they don't, I would still be a suspect."

"Holy shit!"

"Jared, listen to me. I told them I was here last night with you. One of them will be by to talk to you to confirm my story." He stopped now, looked right at me, and I knew what was coming. "Don't tell them everything. I had a hard enough time convincing them that we weren't lovers last summer, and now they'll all know I spent the night here too. Just tell them I came here after we broke up, and I had one too many, and that I didn't want to drive home, and so I crashed on your couch." He looked so scared, and part of me understood, but part of me resented him for it. "Please?"

But then I realized: *Cherie is dead.* Cherie, who obviously wasn't my best friend or anything, but still, I had known her for most of my life. And suddenly it felt awfully petty to begrudge him a little privacy from his coworkers.

"I promise."

IT TURNED out to be the Chief of Police who came to question me.

"So that's it? Officer Richards arrived at your house at around

135

nine o'clock, had a few beers, didn't want to drive home, and slept on your couch the rest of the night?"

It was funny that he was saying, "That's it?" He had been questioning me for more than two hours. "That sums it up, yes."

"So he was sleeping on the *couch?*"

I hated the stupid smirk on his face when he asked that question. What I really wanted to say was, *What does it matter? If he was here, what does it matter if he was on my couch or in my bed?* But I had made a promise.

"Yes."

He looked a little disappointed by the flatness of my response. "Okay, well, I guess that's everything, then. Thank you for your time, Mr. Thomas."

"Chief White, you don't really think that Matt had anything to do with Cherie's death, do you?"

He took a minute to think, debating how much to tell me, but then he sighed and said, "No, not really. One of the neighbors heard a shot, and when she looked out, she saw somebody running away. She thinks it was Dan Snyder, Cherie's ex-husband. It was dark, and she couldn't tell for sure. But certainly the description she gave matches Dan more than it does Officer Richards."

I thought of Dan, who was shorter than me and had a beer gut, and I thought of Matt's tall, muscular body. It would be hard to mistake one for the other.

"That, along with Dan's history of violence toward his ex-wife, makes him a much more likely suspect."

"Then why go to all this trouble?"

"The fact that Matt and Cherie had been dating does mean that we have to question him. If we didn't, it just wouldn't be due diligence. And the fact that he's also a police officer means that we have to be extra careful so as not to show favoritism. We don't want anybody saying that he got away with murder just because he's an officer of the law."

"What about Dan? I assume you're questioning him too?"

"We will, as soon as we find the worthless SOB."

He got up to leave but then stopped at the door, with his hand on the knob. "Son, I know it's none of my business." Oh shit. Nothing good ever came after an opening like that. "I don't know what's going on with you and Matt. I don't know, and I don't really care. But let me tell you, not everybody sees it that way. I was on the force in Denver for fifteen years before I came here. I've seen other gay cops. And it's never easy for them."

He turned and looked at me now. "I don't think you realize how much that boy has gone through for you. He had a hard enough time before this, everybody calling him a queer just because he'd been seen around town with you. But now it's going to get worse. A lot worse."

I had no idea what to say. I could try to deny that anything was going on, yet I knew that wasn't really the point. They were going to think it, whether it was true or not. "Why are you telling me this?"

"I just thought you should know. A time might be coming when Matt has to make a choice. If you care about him—and I think maybe you do— you won't do anything to make that choice harder on him than it already is."

CHAPTER 22

CHERIE'S funeral was a couple of days later. Matt insisted on going together.

"Are you sure that's a good idea?" I asked him. I hadn't seen him since he'd rushed out of my house after hearing about her death, and I hadn't told him about my conversation with Chief White. He just shrugged.

In the movies, it always rains for funerals, but the day of Cherie's funeral was beautiful. Colorado averages over three hundred days of sunshine per year, and this was one of them. The temperature was in the sixties. Only the bare trees and the dead leaves skittering across the ground gave away the season.

Matt stood with me through the funeral and either didn't notice or didn't acknowledge the smirks on the faces of some of his fellow police officers, including Officer Jameson. When it was over, he said, "Let's go say hello."

"Are you crazy?" I snapped.

"Jared." His voice was calm and reasonable. "Just come over, let me introduce you. Shake hands and we'll go."

"No. You go. I'll be in the car."

I could tell he was annoyed, but I didn't care. How could I

smile while he introduced me when I had just seen them elbowing each other over my presence at his side?

We drove back to my place in silence. I thought he was mad about my refusal to meet his coworkers, but as I was about to get out, he said suddenly, "It's my fault she died, isn't it?" He wasn't looking at me but was staring straight ahead through the windshield.

"It's not."

"It is. I was dating her, and he was jealous, and he killed her. And the worst part is I didn't even care about her. I was using her, being a stupid, selfish bastard, and it got her killed."

We both knew that Dan's violence toward Cherie had been increasing for years, and I thought it might have ended the same way with or without Matt. But I also couldn't deny that having Matt as a rival would make any man feel threatened.

"What about Dan? Do you have any idea where he is?"

He seemed to shake off his momentary depression and turned to face me. "No. That bastard never seemed very smart, but he's managed to avoid us so far."

He was still sitting in the Jeep, which surprised me. "Aren't you coming in?"

"Not tonight. I have to go. I had to trade a shift to get the morning off for the funeral. I go in at two, I'm off at ten, but then I have to be back in at six tomorrow."

"Oh." I tried to sound casual, but I felt like he was avoiding being alone with me. "I'll see you later then."

He must have heard something in my voice, because he grabbed my arm and then waited until I looked at him.

"I know what you're thinking, and you're wrong."

"Am I?"

He gave me one of his beautiful smiles and said, "I promise."

THE next night was Thursday, our last tutoring session before the Thanksgiving break, and I only had four kids show up. I ordered pizza again. Between them, they had managed to come up with about seven dollars, which they handed to me proudly.

At this point, I didn't have to help them much. It had become more of a supervised study group, but I was there if they got stuck. I was pretty sure a few of them only came for the social aspect, but I didn't mind.

We were just getting started when Matt knocked on the door.

"You don't have to knock, you know," I told him after I let him in.

He gave me the pseudo-grin. "I'll remember that." He glanced into the dining room, at the kids gathered around the table, and scowled. "I forgot it was Thursday."

"There's pizza on the way."

"How long do they stay?" I was surprised by how annoyed he seemed to be.

"They'll be gone by nine."

He looked over at them again and then pulled me into the hallway where we were out of sight. He wrapped one arm around my waist, pulled me against him, and whispered into my hair, "Can't you make them go home?"

The implications of his questions finally dawned on me, and my body instantly responded. He was holding me tight enough against him that I knew he could feel the effect his words had on me. He moaned a little and backed me against the wall. "Jared, please...."

But just then, the doorbell rang and four teenagers shouted in unison, "Pizza!"

"They have a test tomorrow."

He kissed my neck, just below my ear, and then let go of me. "This is going to be a long two hours, isn't it?" But he was smiling when he said it.

He sat in the living room reading while I helped the kids. I wondered if they could tell how distracted I was. Half the time, I was thinking about what we would be doing once they left. But I hadn't forgotten the warning Chief White had given me, and I was worried that Matt wasn't thinking about the consequences of being with me. Then I would start thinking again about how much I wanted him, and then that would make me feel guilty that maybe *I* wasn't thinking about the consequences of his actions.

The kids finally started packing up their books, getting ready to leave. Matt saw and headed for the bedroom, winking at me as he passed. I knew I was blushing and had to make sure my shirt hung down far enough to cover any signs of my arousal. Luckily, teenagers are remarkably self-absorbed. They were oblivious. I got them out the door and headed for the bedroom. I couldn't believe how nervous I was. My heart was pounding, my palms were sweating, and my stomach was in knots. I stopped first to go to the bathroom and brush my teeth. Whether that was stalling or advance planning, I wasn't sure. Whatever happened, I was determined to let him set the pace. It would be his first time with another man, and I knew there would probably be limits to what he was ready for.

As soon as I walked into the bedroom, he was on me. He kissed me once, urgently, and then he pulled my shirt off and started undoing my pants.

"Matt, are you sure you want to do this?" I had to say it once, now, before the other parts of my body tuned my brain out.

His eyes came up and met mine. "You're asking me that *now*?"

"I just want you to be sure."

His eyes crinkled at me, then he took my face in his hands, and said quietly, "I'm sure."

He kissed me, quick but soft, then pushed me playfully back onto the bed, and pulled my pants off. He took off my boxers and lay down on top of me, still fully clothed. I smiled up at him and tugged on his shirt. "This isn't quite how it works."

He smiled back. "Shhh." His hand was wandering down my side, and he started to kiss my neck. "I still can't believe this is happening." He didn't sound confused or troubled, just surprised. I put my hand on the back of his head and felt the stubbly short hairs there.

"Jared." My name was a quiet whisper against my skin. "I can't get used to feeling like this. I can't believe how much I want you." His lips were soft and warm, and his chin and cheeks were rough with stubble. He moved down to kiss my stomach, moving slowly toward my hip, alternately kissing and biting gently. His mouth never touched my cock. The fact that he was close enough to feel it along his cheek as he kissed me seemed incredible. He worked his way down the sensitive line where my leg met my pelvis, and then all around my patch of hair, tender kisses and his warm tongue leaving a small, wet trail that had me panting beneath him.

He moved back up and kissed my lips once, deep and slow and gentle, and then stood up and began to get undressed. I sat up on the side of the bed to watch him. I wondered if I would ever get used to how beautiful his body was—strong and muscular, his skin smooth and tan. Next to him, I felt scrawny and pale.

He must have seen something on my face, because he cocked his head at me and said teasingly, "Now what?"

I looked him up and down again and said, "I'm suddenly feeling terribly inadequate."

He smiled down at me. "Are you kidding? Don't you have any idea what you do to me?"

I smiled back. There was certainly no doubt, now that he was naked, that this was what he wanted. "I can see, actually."

I grabbed his hips and pulled him over to me. I kissed his stomach first, as he had done to me. The trail of hair leading down from his navel was the sexiest thing I had ever seen. I remembered that night in the tent, months before, when I had been so turned on by the thought of it. Tonight I actually did follow it, first with my fingertips, and then with my lips and tongue. I leaned into that patch of thick, jet black hair at its end. He smelled amazing: musky and masculine and intoxicating.

He was making a low moan deep in his chest, almost like a purr, that was driving me wild, and he had a double fistful of my hair. I put my tongue right at the base of his shaft and slowly ran it up his length, all the way to the salty drop at its tip. I teased my tongue over his slit and then closed my lips over his head, just where the ridge was, and sucked hard. His fingers twitched in my hair, and I heard him moan. I worked my tongue over his slit again, around his rim one more time, and then grabbed his ass with both hands and pulled him toward me so that his cock pushed deep into my mouth. His breath caught, and his hands gripped my head hard, holding me in place for a second, his cock almost gagging me and my nose buried in his thick hair. I thought he was going to come. But suddenly he pulled away, pushing me back gently at the same time.

I looked up, alarmed. "What's wrong?"

"Not that way," he said. He pushed me onto my back and then lay down on top of me. "I want something for both of us this time." He kissed me. It started out tender. His tongue touched mine, and then he sucked at my bottom lip. But it quickly grew more urgent, hungrier. One of his hands went into my hair, and he pulled hard, angling my head back so that he could get to my neck. I ran my hands over his body— first the soft yet prickly stubble of his military short hair, then his strong shoulders and arms, down his back, and around to his stomach, which was perfect, hard and ridged with muscle. My fingers found that tantalizing trail of hairs leading down from his navel. I couldn't stay away from it.

He was still on my neck, licking, kissing, and biting a little. His other hand was roaming over my stomach, down my thigh, then between my legs. His fingers felt everywhere, alternately stroking me and exploring until I thought one more touch might be enough to send me over the edge. I could feel his erection grinding hard against my leg.

I reached into the drawer of the bedside table and found the lube. He stopped kissing my neck and looked worried as he watched me apply some to my rim.

"I didn't mean that," he said quietly.

"You don't want to?" I said it as casually as I could. I didn't want to push him.

"I'm not saying I don't want to. But will that be for both of us?"

I realized what he was asking—would I actually enjoy it too?—and kissed him. "Yes. Trust me."

He relaxed again and went back to my neck, and I was surprised to feel his fingers moving down on my body, past my perineum, gently exploring the area. His fingers starting moving in soft circles around my rim, and I wrapped my arms around him and arched into him, moaning. I heard him say softly in surprise, "Oh," in my ear. Then he whispered, "Tell me what to do."

I had never really been one for giving orders in bed, but I managed to say, "Harder."

The pressure increased, and it felt great, but I really wanted more. I pushed against his hand, wanting to feel his fingers inside me. "More, Matt, please," I whispered. But I felt him tense a little at that, and he shook his head and his hand moved away. Apparently I had found the end of his current comfort zone.

"I don't want to push you," I said to him. "Tell me what you want."

"I don't know!" I was surprised by how frustrated he sounded, but there was a hint of laughter in his voice too. "I want you! Jesus, Jared, I've never been so turned on in my life, but I just have no idea what to do. I feel like I'm in high school all over again." He grinned down at me. "At least there's no stick shift in the way." I laughed at that.

He kissed me, slowly running his tongue over the roof of my mouth and then over my lips, and then he whispered in my ear, "Jared, tell me what to do. Tell me what *you* want."

I knew exactly what I wanted, but I didn't want to freak him out. "You can say no." I hated to sound like a damn porno, but he had asked, right? "I really just want you to fuck me."

He groaned when I said that. His hands tightened on me, and he nodded.

I pushed him up, took the pillow from behind my head and put it under my hips, and maneuvered myself into position, still on my back. He was watching me, stroking himself slowly, and he definitely didn't look like he was bothered by the idea. He put on the condom I handed him without comment. But when I started to push against him, trying to initiate penetration, he hesitated.

"Will I hurt you?" he asked, and I was moved by how much concern I saw in his eyes.

"No. Just go slow at first." That seemed like the right thing to say, but I didn't really expect him to be able to hold back once he started. I was right.

As soon as my body closed around the head of his shaft, his eyes closed, and I felt him shudder. With a groan low in his chest, he

145

pushed the rest of the way in, not hard enough to hurt exactly, but I was glad it wasn't my first time. Then he froze and seemed to be holding his breath as he said, "Oh Jesus, I'm sorry."

"Don't be." It felt wonderful, actually. I was already arching into him, amazed at how well we seemed to fit together. I realized how close I was to coming already.

"Oh my God, that feels incredible," he said. He was holding perfectly still yet trembling with the effort of it.

"For me too. Jesus, Matt, I need you to move. I can't hang on much longer."

"If I move an inch, I'm going to come."

"I think that's the point."

He smiled a little at that and opened his eyes to look down at me. Still, he didn't budge. I took one of his hands, moved it between us to my cock, and pushed against him. That deep purring sound started again in his chest, and he finally relaxed against me and started stroking me off with his hand as he started to thrust. Not deep thrusts, just barely rocking against me, slow and gentle. That exhilarating friction and his strong, rough hand working on me—it was amazing. I reached up and grabbed the headboard with both hands so I could push back and then closed my eyes and let myself get lost in the sensation. It only took a few strokes for me. As soon as my muscles clenched around him, he grabbed me and slammed in hard one last time with a cry that was as much surprise as anything else.

For a minute he stayed there, still inside me, feeling my body spasm around him. Then he pulled out and dropped down on top of me, wrapped both arms tight around me, and became dead weight. For just a fraction of a heartbeat, I thought he had fainted, but then I realized I could hear him whispering, "Oh God. Jared. Wow. Jesus." An endless string of breathless words whispered into my hair.

I turned my chin, kissed his ear and then managed to gasp out,

146

"You're heavy. I can't breathe."

"Sorry."

I pushed hard, and he rolled lazily off of me and lay spread-eagle on his back. "Wow."

I was laughing as I got up and made my way on wobbly legs to the bathroom. I cleaned up and brought the towel back in to him. He still hadn't moved. He looked astounded, blinking at the ceiling. I started wiping him off.

"Can we do that again?" He sounded so earnest that I had to laugh.

"What, already?"

"God, no. I mean, once I can move again."

"When do you think that will be?"

"Maybe by Monday."

I laughed and lay down on my back next to him but with my head on his shoulder. "I'll give you 'til morning."

"I didn't realize it would feel so different."

"Does it? I wouldn't know."

"It was...." He was obviously struggling for a word but settled on, "*Intense.*"

"'Intense' in a good way?"

"In a *very* good way."

I laughed again. "I'm glad you approve."

"And it's good—? I mean, when, um. You know, the other...?"

"Are you asking me if it really is good to be on the receiving end?"

147

"Yes." Obviously relieved that he didn't have to elaborate more.

"It can be, yes. It was just now." I shivered a little, remembering. "Are you worried about it?"

"A little. Well." He laughed nervously. "More than a little, to be honest. But I trust you."

"There's no hurry." But now the rational side of my brain was starting to make noise again. "Matt, are you sure this is what you want?"

"Why are you asking that now? Isn't it what *you* want?" He sounded mostly amused but also a tiny bit exasperated.

"You know it is."

"Then what's the problem?"

So I told him about my conversation with Chief White. But when I was done, he just shrugged. I couldn't see it, but felt his shoulder move under my head.

"You're not worried? A few days ago, you didn't want them to know."

"I know. But I realized something. They all assume we're lovers anyway—that's what they've thought for months now. You have no idea how many times since your birthday they've teased me about our 'lovers' quarrel'. The fact that I was here the other night only reinforced it. The only way to make them *not* think it would be to never see you again. And that's not an option. So if they already assume it's true, and I want it to be true, and you want it to be true— well, I guess I just couldn't see any reason anymore why it shouldn't be true."

"I love your logic."

"I thought you would." I could tell he was smiling even though I couldn't see his face.

"So the Chief's wrong? You don't have to make a choice?"

He turned toward me, nudged me onto my side so that he was tight against my back, and wrapped himself around me like a blanket.

"I've already made it, Jared. He thinks I have to choose just one, either you or my career, but I don't. I choose both." He kissed the back of my neck. "I'm not giving you up for anything. But I'm not quitting my job either."

"Is that really possible?"

"Trust me."

CHAPTER 23

AFTER that, Matt made no effort to hide our relationship. He still had his apartment, but more and more of his things were finding their way to my house, and he spent every night in my bed. I certainly had no complaints about that, but I was surprised to find that I was suddenly the one who wanted to avoid being seen together in public. When we weren't lovers and I knew people might think we were, it hadn't mattered. But now that it was true, I was suddenly embarrassed. I was sure that everybody was staring or whispering about us. I knew it was childish and completely illogical, but I couldn't seem to stop worrying about it. And it wasn't hard to convince him to stay home with me those first few days.

The biggest point of contention, however, quickly became his coworkers. Specifically, my unwillingness to meet them or spend time with them.

"Jared, just meet them," he said on more than one occasion.

"Why would I want to meet them? I know what they think of me."

"I know it will be awkward at first, but it will help in the long run."

"No!" I couldn't believe he expected me to subject myself to their derision.

That exchange began to take on the repetition of a broken record.

Of course we went to Lizzy and Brian's for Thanksgiving dinner. The minute Matt walked in the door, Lizzy flew at him and threw her arms around him with a squeal.

"Oh Matt, it's so good to see you!"

"You, too, Lizzy."

"I told Jared you would pull your head out of your ass eventually!"

He turned bright red but said, "Right, as usual."

She beamed at him.

Brian brought James in and started to hand him to Matt. Matt's reaction was the same as mine had been.

"I can't hold him! What if I drop him?"

"You won't."

James looked tiny in Matt's big hands. Matt sat on the couch holding him for a while. He unwrapped him and checked all of his fingers and toes. He brushed his fingers over James's cheek and smiled when James turned his head toward them, his tiny lips making suckling sounds.

"He's so tiny."

"Yes." Lizzy rubbed her hand on the top of Matt's head. "Are you going to help Jared watch him on our date night?"

"You bet."

"Then I hereby name you an honorary uncle. Uncle Matt."

He gave her his dazzling smile. "I like the sound of that."

THE day of my meeting with the high school committee arrived. I made an effort to look a little more respectable than usual. I spent a ridiculously long time trying to get all of my curls back into a ponytail and wore the one pair of slacks that I owned and a button-up shirt and tie.

"Wow." Matt said when I came out of the bedroom. "You're really pulling out all the stops. Are you nervous?"

"Very."

"It will be fine. I'll have a beer open for you when you get back."

I felt like I was going off to war, and I was armed for battle. I had thought it over and decided that I was going to fight them. I took a copy of my teacher's certificate with me and the supportive letters I had received from some of the parents. If the parents wanted me to tutor their kids, why did the school have to get involved at all?

Walking into the high school was strange. I hadn't been there since I was a student fifteen years earlier, but it seemed like nothing had changed. The mural on the wall was the same; the strange speckled linoleum was the same. Even the weird smell was the same. I felt sure that I could walk up to my old locker and open it up, and my books would still be sitting there waiting for me. It brought back all those feelings from my high school years of trying to hide what I knew I was. It didn't help my confidence any.

The "committee" consisted of four people. Mr. Stevens, the band director, was one of them. Alice Rochester started to make introductions, and I was surprised that they were assuming we were all on a first-name basis.

"This is Ann, our math teacher." Alice indicated a small blonde woman, younger than me, who probably had every one of her male students wrapped around her finger. "And Roger, our science teacher." About my age, but short and pudgy. "And I think you know Bill, our band instructor." Of course he was wearing a bow tie. I shook hands all around and then sat in the chair they had left for me.

"Jared," Alice began, "we've been hearing a lot about you lately. Several of our students have been talking, and we've had a few calls from parents too."

"Look, if this is about the tutoring, I have notes from the parents, and I have my teaching certificate—"

"You brought it with you? Oh good! I meant to ask. So, I take it you know why you're here?"

"I assume it's because somebody thinks that I can't tutor a few kids without acting like a damn pedophile and groping a few of them, but I assure you—"

Suddenly there was a lot of fidgeting and paper rustling, and everybody was looking up at the ceiling, appearing very flustered. Everybody except Mr. Stevens. "Jared," he said kindly, "I'm afraid you have greatly misconstrued the purpose of this meeting."

"I have?"

"Would I be here if the agenda was simply to persecute you for your sexual orientation?"

"Um...." I felt like an idiot. I looked around at everybody. Alice and Roger were still fidgeting and looking somewhere over my head, but Ann was smiling at me. "Jesus. I'm sorry." Why can't I ever keep my mouth shut? I couldn't have just waited to see what they had to say before I started raving at them? I took a couple of deep breaths, and when I looked around again, I was relieved to see that they had started to look at me again. "Boy, this is embarrassing. Listen, how about I just shut up, and we can start over?"

Alice gave me her toothpaste commercial smile again. "Jared, I had no idea you were expecting to be attacked when you came in here, although it does clarify parts of our conversation the other day." Just when I thought I couldn't be more embarrassed. "I should have been clearer. The reason we asked you to come here today is this: we'd like to offer you a position here at the school."

And if she had told me that she was going to strip naked and jump off the building, I wouldn't have been more surprised. "You mean, like a job?"

"Yes. 'Like a job'." Her mouth twisted into a lopsided grin, and I think she almost winked when she said that. "The truth is, Jared, most of our teachers are overloaded right now. They're teaching more subjects than they can handle, and many of them are teaching subjects which they never specialized in. The higher math and science classes especially have been, um, a little bit problematic."

"What Alice is too nice to say," Ann cut in, "is that Roger and I don't know what the hell we're doing." Alice started to protest, but Ann cut her off. "It's true. I never intended to be a math teacher. That's just how things ended up. I can teach the lower level classes fine, but the truth is, advanced algebra and calculus are over my head." She looked over at Roger.

He nodded. "It's true. I'm a biologist. And I can manage with chemistry. But physics is beyond me."

Alice started again now. "Ann and Roger have been doing their best, but the fact is it's a terrible disservice to the students." Nods all around.

Ann spoke again. "We don't have that many students who make it to calculus or who want to take physics, but there are a few. So many of them struggle, and I've never been able to help them much." I remembered Ringo saying his teacher didn't know anything. I hadn't realized he was right. "But all of a sudden, this year, students started getting A's. They started catching *me* making mistakes." She was turning red. "That's not fun in a class of high school kids, let me tell you. And it wasn't long before we started hearing all about you."

"So, you want me to teach?" I knew that was a stupid question, but I couldn't seem to wrap my brain around it. I had been so sure that I was walking into a battle. I still hadn't quite recovered.

"The position would start in January, at midterm. I've put together a package for you with information on benefits and pay. We can't pay you much. You could make more teaching in Boulder or Fort Collins, but since you already have a home here in Coda, we thought maybe we could convince you." She handed me a folder filled with papers. "Take some time to think about it and talk it over with your family. Feel free to call me with any other questions in the meantime."

"The fact that I'm gay isn't a problem?"

It was Mr. Stevens who answered, and I realized he had probably been included in this meeting specifically for this reason. "It's not a problem as far as the school is concerned. I can't lie to you—there will be parents who will complain. Not many, but a few. However, the fact remains that, like band, physics, advanced algebra, and calculus are all electives. So parents can decide. If their personal prejudices are more important than the furthering of their children's education, well, frankly, it's not our problem. I'm not going to lie to you, Jared. It's not always easy. Kids can be mean and so can their parents. But it can also be very rewarding."

"I, uh...." I wasn't exactly being articulate. "I'm really sorry about earlier. I had no idea. I really don't know what to say."

"Well, we hope you'll say 'yes.'"

CHAPTER 24

SOME rational part of my brain knew that I should be thrilled about the job. But the rest of my brain, which seemed to be the bigger part, felt nothing but anxiety. I couldn't really put my finger on the source of that anxiety. Partly it was the shop and knowing that I would be putting Brian and Lizzy in a bad spot. Part of it was the knowledge that some parents wouldn't like it. Part of it was my own memory of the things that had been said about Mr. Stevens by some of my fellow students back when I was in school. Was there more to it than that? I wasn't sure. I only knew that the very thought of taking the job had me breaking out in a cold sweat.

Matt was overjoyed when I told him. He actually picked me up in a bear hug that had my ribs aching.

"That's amazing! And you thought they wanted to chew you out. Are you going to call Lizzy?"

The thought of telling Lizzy was nauseating. "Not right now."

"Can I call her?"

I couldn't even look at him when I answered. "No."

"Why not?" and the happiness in his voice had been replaced by confusion.

"Because, I don't know yet if I'm going to take the job."

"*What?*"

"Which part of that sentence confused you, Matt?" I had meant that as a joke, but it came out sounding snarkier than I intended.

"Fine." And now he sounded hurt and angry.

"Let's just make dinner, okay? We can talk about it later?"

I was still avoiding going out with him. He flinched a little every time I insisted on making dinner at home and his eyes got a little darker, but we never argued about it.

We did, however, argue again about his coworkers and my continued refusal to spend time with them. And that night over dinner, he dropped the Christmas bombshell on me.

"Jared, the department is hosting a Christmas party in a couple of weeks, and I really want you to come with me." He didn't expect me to agree. I could tell he was already braced for a fight. And with good reason.

I kept my eyes on my plate. "No way."

"That's it? 'No way'? You won't even consider it?" I could tell he was fighting to keep his voice even. He never yelled—I think he consciously chose to not act like his father— but his voice would get low and dangerous.

"I don't need to consider it to know I'll be miserable."

"I'm going to be miserable too."

I looked up at him and attempted to smile. "Exactly. So let's stay home."

"Jared, that's not the answer. We have to be together. We have to make them face it. Eventually it won't seem like such a big deal to them anymore."

"Do you really think shoving it in their faces is the solution?"

"Nobody is 'shoving' anything in anyone's face. You think

I'm going to fuck you on the buffet table or something?" His voice was quiet and tight, like he was carefully controlling every consonant, every syllable a struggle. He was seriously pissed at me now. "I'm not an idiot. All I'm saying is they have to get used to seeing us together."

"So I'm supposed to just stand there, pretending to have fun, while they point and laugh?"

"Maybe, yes."

"No. Fucking. Way."

That was the first night we went to bed still mad. I lay on my side of the bed, miserable, listening to him breathing on the other side. I knew he was still awake. I wanted so much to touch him, to bridge that gap. But there was nothing I could say that would fix it short of giving in, which I wasn't prepared to do.

It went on for days. I knew in the back of my mind that this should have been a happy time for us. And at times it was. We watched football and we made love a lot. But most of the rest of our time seemed to be taken up by arguments over those two points of contention: my job offer and his fellow police officers. 'Round and 'round we went, and we didn't seem to be getting anywhere.

It all came to a head one night at Lizzy's house. She had invited us over for dinner. We argued for an hour before we got there about whether or not I should tell Lizzy and Brian about the job. Of course, he thought I should. But I didn't want to cause trouble until I had made a decision.

We were snapping at each other from the minute we walked in the door. Everybody tried to pretend like they didn't notice, but I knew they did. Dinner was quiet and awkward. We were just finishing up when Brian said, "Jared, we need to talk about the shop." He looked nervous when he said it, and Lizzy was staring at her plate. Matt perked up but didn't say anything.

"Sure. What's up?"

"Now that Lizzy's been home with the baby for a few weeks, she's having second thoughts about coming back to work."

"Oh."

"I know it's been tough for you without her. You're working long hours. And Ringo can't help much, except on the weekends."

"It's okay—"

"Tell them," Matt said, quietly enough that only I heard him.

I ignored him. "I can handle it."

"No, you can't, Jared," Mom said gently. "You can't do it by yourself."

"You'll want days off and vacations," Lizzy interjected.

"Ringo will graduate next spring—" I started to say.

"Tell them," Matt said a little more forcefully. Lizzy's eyes darted to him curiously, but nobody else seemed to notice.

"Jared," Brian interrupted, "he's not going to stay. You know that. He'll be going off to college. We could hire another high school student to help out, but it still won't solve the problem."

"Then what do you suggest?" I asked him.

"Well, we can look at the possibility of letting Ringo go and hiring a full time employee."

"We can't afford that. Especially since a full-time employee would expect benefits."

"Maybe it's time to think about selling it."

"No—"

"Tell them!" This time it was loud enough that they couldn't ignore him.

"No!" I hissed at him.

"Tell us what, Jared?" Lizzy asked with a challenge in her blue eyes.

"It's nothing!" I told her and then turned to him. "Not now!" I couldn't believe how angry I suddenly was at him. We had been arguing about it for days, and the fact that he would try to force my hand pissed me off to no end.

But he was staring right back at me, and he looked just as mad. "It's not 'nothing'!" He kept his gaze level on mine and said, "Jared has been offered a full-time job teaching at the high school next semester."

"What?" Brian said.

"That's great!" Mom said.

"Why didn't you tell us?" Lizzy asked.

I barely heard any of them. "You incredible fucking bastard! I can't believe you just did that!"

"Why not? I've been trying to get you to tell them for the last week—"

"*What?*" Lizzy sounded pissed now too.

"You knew I didn't want to say anything." My voice was getting louder.

His, on the other hand, was getting lower, his words clipped short as he got angrier. "And you don't think that your job offer is relevant to this discussion?"

"You had no right!"

"I had *no right*? What the fuck is that supposed to mean?"

And now I really was yelling. "You had *no right* because it's none of your goddamn business!"

Everybody froze. I saw in his steel-gray eyes all of the doors slamming shut in a way I hadn't seen in months. His gaze turned icy, his face guarded and expressionless. "So that's how it is. I can't believe I didn't realize sooner."

He stood up and started to walk away.

"What the hell is that supposed to mean?" I made an effort not to yell, tried to keep my voice level. Almost succeeded. Brian was looking terribly uncomfortable. Lizzy looked pissed as hell, and I had a feeling it was at me. I couldn't tell what Mom was thinking.

"It means I should have realized what was going on. You've drawn a line, haven't you? And I'm not supposed to cross it. And apparently that line is just outside the bedroom door!" Brian jumped up and grabbed whatever dishes were closest to him and took them into the kitchen. Mom and Lizzy didn't move. Matt wasn't done. "You talk a pretty good game, but the fact is, you're still ashamed of who you are, and you're ashamed to be with me!"

"I'm not!"

"You are! Don't act like you don't know what I'm talking about. You think I haven't noticed that suddenly we can't even go out to eat anymore? Sure, you're fine with being gay, but only because you live your life in a fucking bubble! As soon as it comes down to actually facing people, you bury your head in the sand."

"That's not fair!"

"*Fair*? Do you have any idea what I put up with at work for you? Have you ever even thought about it? Do you think that's 'fair'? I ask you to make just a little bit of an effort for me, and you won't even consider it. And *you* have the nerve to talk to *me* about 'fair'? You said this was what you wanted, but now you're the one who can't face it!"

"Wait—" I was backpedaling now.

But he ignored me and kept talking. "And now this job! I've seen you with those kids. I know how much you love teaching them. But you're going to pass up a chance to teach full time just so you

161

can avoid having to deal with a few bigoted parents or a few asshole teenagers. You're going to keep working at that shop for the rest of your life, just so you don't have to face the rest of the world. You can tell yourself that it's because you have to. That it's because your family needs you to. But it's bullshit, Jared! The real reason you won't consider it is because you're scared."

"Are you done?" I asked icily.

"Yeah. I'm definitely done with this whole fucked-up situation." He turned and walked out, and I heard the front door slam.

Lizzy jumped up and threw a roll at my head. Her aim was impeccable. "Asshole!" She ran after Matt.

Only Mom and I were left. I put my head in my hands on the table. I was shaking, terrified that his last statement meant he was leaving me for good. I wanted to chase after him, but then what? I couldn't do what he wanted me to do, but I couldn't bear to lose him either. I was still pissed, but I was also fighting hard to keep from bursting into tears.

Mom was quiet for a long time, but I knew she would say something eventually. If she didn't have something to say, she would have left the table already. Finally, she took a deep breath and said, "Jared, let me say two things, and then I'll never mention this ugly incident again."

"Do I have a choice?"

"No, you don't. The first is this: you can't control what others think. The only thing you can control is yourself. Some people will look down on you for your choices in life, no matter what they are. You can't do anything about that. The only thing you can do is decide how to live your own life. And to hell with everybody else.

"The second is this: I know being in a committed relationship is new for you. But trust me on this: you can't just pick tiny pieces of yourself to share, and keep the rest to yourself. It doesn't work that way. It's all or nothing.

"Third—"

"You said there were only two things."

"I lied. The third thing is simply this." She put her hand on my shoulder, and that gentle touch made me lose my battle to keep the tears back. I let them come and was childishly relieved that only my mother was there to see it. Her voice was soft when she continued. "That boy loves you. Don't be such a pigheaded fool that you can't see it."

She kissed me on the back of my head and left.

Lizzy gave me a ride home in stony silence. I had no idea what had passed between her and Matt after she followed him out of the dining room. I only knew that she came back hurt and angry and he didn't come back at all. She parked in front of my house, but when I started to get out, she finally broke the silence.

"Why didn't you tell me?"

I rested my forehead against the cool glass of the window. I couldn't look at her. "I don't know."

"I thought we were friends."

"We are, Lizzy."

"Really?" She sniffled a little, and when I looked over, there were tears on her face. I couldn't remember ever feeling like such an ass.

"Yes, Lizzy." I reached over and took her hand. "You know I love you. I don't know why I didn't tell you. I know that's a ridiculously lame answer, but it's true. I just didn't want anybody to know. The thought of taking that job ties my stomach in knots, and I can't really explain why. Maybe he's right. Maybe I'm just scared." Now that I had said it, I had to really examine it and I didn't like what I saw.

She was quiet for a minute but finally said, "Jared, don't worry about the shop. We'll figure something out. Take the job."

"I don't know, Lizzy—"

"*Take the job*. And pull your head out your ass. You owe Matt an apology."

It wasn't until I got in the house that I realized Matt wasn't there. I tried calling his apartment but hung up when his voice mail picked up. I debated driving over but decided that would just be asking for trouble. I was sure he was still angry. I was, too, but only a little. Mostly I was hurt and ashamed. I knew if I tried to talk to him now, he would still be in attack mode and I would be defensive, and in the end, we would probably only end up saying more things we didn't mean.

The next morning I called again and got his voice mail. This time I left a message. "Matt, I'm sorry. Please come home."

I kept remembering what it had been like after my birthday, leaving messages for him and never hearing back. I spent the whole day at work trying to convince myself that he wouldn't do that to me again. I was hopelessly relieved when I got home and found him waiting for me. He was sitting on one of the stools at the breakfast bar. He looked scared but also determined. I was so glad to see him and started to go to him, but he held up his hand to stop me.

"Stay over there." He wasn't looking at me, but his voice was firm.

"Why?"

"I have something I need to say to you. If you're here, where I can touch you...." He took a deep breath and then looked up at me. "I'll lose my nerve."

I was sure my heart had stopped beating. There was only one thing that could make him sound so cold and so final while looking so scared. I leaned against the door, tried to steady my breathing, and waited for him to tell me that he was leaving me forever—leaving me alone again. I felt my arms cross over my chest and hugged myself tight, hoping I could keep myself together and knowing it was futile. I was sure that I would fly into a thousand pieces and be lost forever if he left me.

He took another deep breath and started talking. "I don't do things halfway. Once I make a decision, I generally don't waste time second-guessing myself. And with the exception of one very bad decision I made a couple of months ago"—he blushed when he said this, and I knew he was talking about his decision to leave me and date Cherie—"it has always been for the best." He stopped for a minute, but I knew he wasn't finished, so I waited. "So when I made the decision to be with you, I just assumed that what you wanted and what I wanted were the same thing. But I realize now that I should have asked you."

My mind was scrambling for purchase, trying to see where this was headed. Maybe I was wrong. Maybe he wasn't breaking up with me. I hardly dared to hope. "You knew what I wanted." I barely managed to get the words out.

He shook his head. "I thought I did. I assumed I did. But I never asked. I assumed that this"—he indicated the two of us—"was going to be something serious. I basically moved in with you, and I never stopped to question if that was what you wanted."

"It was, Matt." I hated how desperate I sounded. "It *is*."

"Are you sure, Jared?" I started to answer, but he held up his hand to stop me. "Don't talk. Let me finish. This relationship isn't easy for me. It's going to take time for the guys at the department to get used to the idea of me being gay. I mean, I'm still getting used to the idea myself. I've spent the last few months denying that we were lovers, and now suddenly I'm not denying it, and they know that I've been living here, and I have to take a lot of shit for that. The truth is, Jared, I'm willing to deal with it, because of the way I feel about you. Because I'm not happy unless I'm with you. But I'm not sure I'm willing to deal with it if all you're interested in is sex. I know that sounds like an ultimatum, and I don't want it to, but I have to be honest. I want us to be together. But, like I said, I don't do things halfway. So if we're together, I need it to be for real. I need you to be sure."

He stopped short like he wasn't done but wasn't sure what else to say. I felt like I was gasping for air, flooded with relief at what I was hearing. Once I had my balance, I looked back up at him. He was still sitting there, looking lost, looking like he needed to say more but didn't know how. When it became evident he wasn't going to say anything else, I asked, "Can I talk now?"

He almost smiled. "Yes."

I went to him, put my arms around him, and kissed him, just barely. "Matt, this *is* what I want. I *do* want you here with me. It's not just about sex. I'm crazy about you, and there's nothing I want more than for us to be together."

He looked relieved but still did not reach for me. "Jared, I don't want to fight anymore. We need to decide *now* how we're going to handle this."

I took a deep breath. This was the part I wasn't sure about. "Okay."

"I know you're embarrassed—"

"Not of you."

He ignored my interruption. "And I understand, to a certain extent. But, I think you're going about it wrong, trying to hide it. We can spend our lives holed up here in this house, trying to pretend like we're not together, but in a town this small, people will still know. And they *will* talk. And it seems to me that acting like criminals will only give them more to gossip about. I'm not saying it's easy for me either, Jared, but I don't want to hide anymore. I will not spend the rest of my life being ashamed of my love for you."

That was the first time he had ever used that word, and I was stunned into silence. Only a few minutes ago, I had been sure that he was leaving me, and now he was actually saying that he loved me.

"Jared, please say something."

My voice was shaking as I asked, "You really love me?"

He put one hand in my hair and pulled me closer, smiling and shaking his head at me. "Do you really have to ask?"

Some knot in my chest that I hadn't quite realized still existed loosened up and was gone. He loved me, and he really was happy with me, despite everything that it cost him with his coworkers. Was it really so much to ask for me to try to make it easier? I was causing all of these arguments, but why? Because I was too proud to face his coworkers? It occurred to me how proud I should be that he wanted me with him. I closed my eyes and concentrated on not allowing myself to cry in front of him, but I couldn't stop my breath from shaking.

"What is it, Jared?" His voice was so gentle. "Talk to me."

"You were right—I am scared. But...." I opened my eyes again and looked into his. "I don't want to fight anymore either. I'll do whatever you want me to do."

He smiled again and then kissed me gently. "Will you go riding with me tomorrow?"

That simple request surprised me. "Of course."

"Two of the guys from the station will be there."

"Oh."

"But you'll go?"

This was it. I couldn't turn back now. "If you want me to."

"Will you go to the party with me on Saturday?"

My pulse raced, and I felt butterflies in my stomach just

thinking about it. "I will. I'll hate it, but I'll go if that's what you want."

"It is." He tightened his arm around me and kissed me again, and then the hand in my hair pulled a little, like I knew it would, angling my head to the side so he could kiss my cheek, then my jaw, and then my neck. His voice was low and full of a promise that made my knees go weak as his lips brushed my ear. "Will you come in the bedroom with me?"

I laughed with relief. "God, yes. Happily."

He led me to the bedroom and slowly, slowly, undressed me, kissing me everywhere. He took nothing for himself, gently turning away all of my efforts to please him, and used his hands and his mouth on me, teasing me into the most amazing orgasm I had experienced in a long time. And afterward, he kissed me gently, held me tight against him, and whispered in my ear, "I do love you, Jared. It frightens me sometimes how much I love you."

I could not stop the tears this time and was relieved that it was dark in the bedroom, so he couldn't see them. I put my arms around him. "Matt—"

He silenced me with a finger on my lips. "Shh." He wrapped himself around me, chest to chest, legs tangled together, one hand moving through my hair. He kissed my forehead. "No more talking, Jared. Just let me hold you."

Any doubts I might have had were gone. He loved me. Nothing else mattered.

CHAPTER 25

THE next day, just after lunch, we loaded our bikes onto the Jeep and headed for the trailhead. I was leaning against the window, watching the trees fly past, trying to steady my nerves and convince myself that I didn't really need to throw up. I hated myself for being so nervous.

"Are you okay over there?" Matt asked lightly.

"No. I'm trying to remember why I agreed to this." I was trying to remember our conversation from the day before, but in the harsh light of day, it was hard to hang on to. I forced myself to remember his whisper in my ear, his arms tight around me, as he told me that he loved me. That's why I was here. I was doing this for him. Still, it was doing nothing to alleviate the knots in my stomach.

"It's going to be fine."

"That's easy for you to say." Logically, I knew that he was right. It was just riding, which I love. I probably wouldn't have to talk to them much at all. And in a few short hours, we would be back home. I took a deep breath. "Who are these guys? What should I expect?"

"Grant Jameson and Tyson McDaniels."

It took me a second to figure out why that name sounded

familiar. "Grant Jameson? That asshole that came to my house and asked if I had kids in my bedroom?"

"Grant *is* an asshole. I won't even try to deny it. But Tyson is an okay guy. Mostly he just follows Grant's lead. I think if he knows you better, maybe he'll quit listening to Grant so much. Grant will probably always harass me about it, but it's starting to be more like *friendly* harassment. Most of the time, at least. And I think it's important for them to realize that I'm not ashamed to be with you."

"So they accept you now but not me, even though they know we're together?"

"For the most part. Once they realized that calling me names wasn't going to change anything and that I could still hold my own against any of them, they got over it." He shrugged. "Mostly. Some of the older cops will never accept me, and I can deal with that. But Grant and Tyson are the ones I work with the most, and I need for them to get used to it. They're starting to accept it, especially Tyson. They know me, and I don't fit their stereotype. You don't fit it either, but you refuse to prove it."

"That's really all it takes?" I was still skeptical.

"I think that's a lot of it, yes."

I shook my head. "I think you're kidding yourself." He didn't answer, and we drove a while in silence. I was confused when he passed the turnoff for the trail we usually rode. "Where're we going?"

"Johnson's Rock."

That surprised me. Johnson's Rock was the toughest trail in the area. Matt could almost keep up with me on the easier trails, but the one time we had tried Johnson's Rock, he had struggled more than usual.

"Why?"

"It seemed like a good idea."

"Are these guys that good?"

He smiled over at me. "Not even close."

"You do realize you're making no sense at all, right?"

"I told them the other day that you and I were going riding. And Grant asked, wouldn't I rather ride with somebody who could keep up with me instead of a fucking fairy? So I suggested that they come with us."

"That's why we're going to the toughest trail in the area?"

"Exactly!"

"I still don't see how this will change anything."

"It's all about competition. They have respect for people who can beat them."

The light came on. "Ah. I think it's all making sense now."

"It will bring Grant down a notch to eat your dust all day. And it will prove to them both that you're not what they expect."

"You are a manipulative bastard."

"I am." And the smile he gave me made up for it all.

Grant and Tyson were waiting for us at the trailhead. Tyson nodded and shook my hand when Matt introduced me, although he seemed unwilling to meet my eyes. Grant didn't even acknowledge my existence.

We mounted up and were just ready to start out, when Grant said, "Are you boys and *girls* ready?" Tyson turned away, obviously embarrassed. Matt ignored him completely. I felt myself go red up to my hairline and heard the blood pounding in my ears, but I kept my eyes on the ground and said nothing. "Okay then," Grant said when it became obvious nobody was going to respond. "I'll wait for you at the top."

Matt smiled at him. "We'll see who's waiting for who,

171

asshole." He said it jokingly, and Grant and Tyson both laughed before starting out, leaving Matt and me at the trailhead.

"You ready?" he asked me.

I couldn't even look at him. "I'm trying not to hate you right now."

He put his hand on the back of my neck and waited until my eyes met his. "I know." Then he leaned over and kissed me lightly. "Thank you for trusting me."

I shook my head but let it go and asked instead, "Do you want me to wait for you? And them?"

"Only if you want to."

We finally started out. I left Matt behind me and passed Grant and Tyson within minutes. Once I was off on my own, my bad mood started to wear off. I love it all too much, the mountains and the riding and the challenge of making it up the trail. The sun was shining. The temperature was in the low fifties, but the breeze had a hint of frost in it. Among the towering evergreens were patches of aspen, their white limbs bare. Sheltered patches of ground that never saw the sun had snow that wouldn't melt until next spring. I found that I couldn't hang on to my anger.

I turned around and rode back down to them. Matt was riding with them now.

"Hey," he said happily as I reached them. "Is it a successful ride? Are you bleeding yet?"

I laughed. "Not yet. Are you?"

"Only Tyson, so far. We were just talking about a bet— whoever crashes the least has to buy dinner."

I couldn't help but smile back at him. "You're on."

I rode with them for a few minutes until we got to the next hard section, where I ended up ahead of them again without meaning to. The rest of the ride was like that. I would ride ahead for a while, on my own, and then turn around and ride back down to meet them. We would ride together for a while, but I always seemed to end up out front on my own after a while, whether I meant to or not.

"Jesus, Jared," Tyson said once as I rode back down to them. "You've probably ridden twice as far as us. Aren't you exhausted?"

"No, but I'm pretty fucking hungry," I said jokingly. "I wish you guys would hurry the hell up." Tyson laughed. Grant just shook his head at me. Matt was smiling at me like I had hung the fucking sun and moon, which somehow had me annoyed at him but ridiculously pleased at the same time.

Eventually, Matt left them, too, and rode with me to the top. We took a short break and then headed back down. We found Grant and Tyson resting where we had left them. "Aren't you guys going up?" Matt asked.

"Hell, no," Grant said. "We're beat."

It was easier to stay together on the way down, and I only finished a few minutes ahead of them.

"Good ride, guys." Matt said when they finally reached us. "Next time we'll pick an easy trail so you pansies can keep up."

Tyson actually laughed. "Looks like dinner is on Jared."

"I crashed too," I said. Since I had only been with them about half the time, I wasn't really sure who had won the bet.

"Don't think you can get out of it by acting humble," Grant said, surprising me. Not only was it the first time he had spoken to me directly, but he even sounded halfway civil. "You rode circles around us all day. You're buying!"

"You bet," Matt answered for me. "We'll meet you at Tony's." And if his smile got any bigger I thought I might have to punch him.

"Will you please quit looking so damn pleased with yourself?" I said as we drove down, although I found that I was smiling a little too.

"Eventually. Admit it—it was a good idea."

"I guess."

"It's okay to admit that I'm right, you know." He winked over at me. "Just say it. Say, 'You're right, Matt'."

I rolled my eyes at him. "You really, truly are a manipulative bastard. And you *might* be right. That's all you're getting." He laughed.

So we had dinner with Grant and Tyson. Mostly the three of them talked shop and I just listened. They were still looking for Dan Snyder, but after checking with all of his relatives, they had nothing to go on. We did talk about football and mountain biking a little. Tyson was friendly from the beginning, but by the end, even Grant had loosened up, and when we started to leave, he stopped me. He waited until Matt and Tyson were a few steps ahead and then said nervously, without actually looking at me, "Look, no hard feelings, okay?" He held his hand out, and I shook it, hoping I didn't look as amazed as I felt.

Matt and I drove home in silence. We had barely made it through the front door of our house when he tackled me and pinned me to the floor. It didn't take much effort on his part, and I wondered just how good he had been at wrestling in high school.

"Oh my God, you're heavy!"

"Say it again! I just want to hear you say it one more time!"

"You're heavy!"

"Not that. Come on now."

"You're a manipulative bastard."

"Try again."

174

"You were right! Is that what you wanted to hear, you huge oaf?"

"Exactly!" He smiled down at me, that amazing smile that could still make me melt. "You should be getting used to that by now."

"How long are you going to gloat?" I asked him jokingly.

"I haven't decided yet." He was still on top of me, but it had turned into more of an embrace, and I could feel him unbuttoning my pants with his free hand. He started kissing my neck, and I slid my hands under his shirt, up his back. "Now what about the job?" he asked quietly, his lips soft against my skin. "Will you take it? I'm right about that, too, you know."

I sighed. I knew I would have to face it soon, but not quite yet. Not this moment. All I wanted at this moment was him. The fumbling below had shifted now, and I knew he was undoing his own pants. "I'll think about it. Is that enough for now?"

He was smiling when he said, "For now."

I reached down and slid his pants and briefs down over his hips. I couldn't get them far, but they were at least out of the way. He reached into my boxers and pulled my cock out so that it was lined up against his, wrapped his hand around both of us, and started to pump his hand slowly up and down.

Despite his enthusiasm for sex that first day, we had only fucked one other time, and even then, only because I wanted it. At first I thought he was embarrassed, but then I started to realize that the act itself made him uncomfortable. When I tried to ask him about it, he simply said, "It isn't fair to you."

I tried to convince him that I didn't mind being bottom every time, at least for now, but it didn't help.

"Do you think less of me, for letting it be done to me?" I had asked him.

"No. Not at all." I wasn't sure if it was true, or if he only wanted it to be true.

"Then what?"

"How can *you* not think less of *me* afterwards?"

That didn't make any sense to me, but I didn't push. After all, it had barely been a month since his first sexual experience with another man. I figured whatever his hang-up was, he would get over it in time. For now, we had other ways of pleasing each other. Still, I was surprised to discover that this was actually what he liked best: holding our cocks together and beating us off at the same time. He said it was because he could watch me. I tried not to be self conscious after that, but I also thought it was because he could kiss me easier. Whatever his reason, I wasn't going to object.

I put my hand over his and urged him to pump faster. He had developed a sort of twist at the top of each stroke that caused the heads of our cocks to rub sideways against each other, just a tiny bit, and it was fantastic. Still, he had taken care of me the night before. For him, it had been several days, and it was only a minute or two before his fist was slick from his own come.

He moved down then. Whatever his hang-ups about anal sex, he had none whatsoever about getting come in his mouth. I put my hands on his head, doing my best not to push, while he sucked. However, I couldn't stop my hips from thrusting up toward him when I came, and he groaned, too, not from discomfort, as I unloaded in his mouth.

I was still reeling from my orgasm when he moved up and kissed me. "I hope you know," he whispered into my ear as he nuzzled my neck, "that was only a warmup."

CHAPTER 26

THE Christmas party turned out to be not as bad as I had expected. A couple of the older cops pointedly ignored us, but Tyson and his wife seemed to make an effort to stand by me most of the evening, and while Grant wasn't exactly friendly, he wasn't a complete jerk either.

The next week, I had one last tutoring session with the kids. I had a full house, as they were all preparing for finals. Several of the parents had sent money along to cover the cost of the pizza. I was surprised when the doorbell rang that, instead of answering it, Matt came into the dining room and said to me, "You better get that."

I could hear him talking to the kids but didn't think much of it. I paid for the pizza and then stopped in the kitchen for paper plates and napkins. As soon as I stepped back into the dining room, the kids erupted into cheers. Two of the girls jumped up and threw their arms around me. One was squealing into my ear loud enough that I feared I would have permanent hearing loss. Matt ducked his head and quickly left the room. The rest of the kids were coming over now and shaking my hand or hugging me or pounding me on the back.

"What's this about?" I asked as I tried to pry one of the girls off of me.

"We just heard you're going to be our teacher next semester!" Ringo said, and then they all started talking at once.

"It will be so great—"

"You're the best—"

"Why didn't you tell us?"

"Wait!" Of course, Matt's odd behavior made sense now. Talk about throwing me to the wolves. I had to wait a second for all the commotion to die down before saying, "I haven't actually accepted the offer yet."

"But you will, right?"

"We'll see." They all started to talk again at once. "Stop! Whether I take the job or not, you guys still have finals to study for, so get back to work."

I found Matt in the kitchen. He was staring at the floor, cheeks red, looking incredibly guilty. He kept his head down but glanced up at me.

"Are you mad?"

"I should be."

"But are you?"

I thought about it and realized that I wasn't at all. What I felt was actually more like relief. At some point over the last week, I had made the decision to trust his judgment, and I felt good about it. The nagging anxiety which had been eating away at me ever since that fateful meeting earlier in the month had faded to nothing more than a few frantic butterflies in my stomach. Mom's advice about deciding how to live seemed to magically make a little more sense. And the reaction of the students—*my* students—had decided it for me.

"I'll call tomorrow and accept the job." That made him smile. "You really are a manipulative bastard. I've told you that before, right?"

He grabbed my shirt and pulled me over to him. "Just say it one more time."

"You're a manipulative bastard."

"Not *that*. You know what you're supposed to say."

"You were right."

He laughed. "I'll never get tired of hearing that."

A FEW days later, Cole called.

"Hey, Sweets!" he said in his lilting, flirtatious voice. "I'm back in Vail. Want some company tonight?"

"Sorry, Cole. I can't." Matt was on the couch reading, and his head jerked up when I said that name.

"You can't *tonight*, or you can't because of a certain tall, dark, very angry-looking police officer?"

"The latter."

"Closet door wasn't locked after all?"

"I guess I found the key." Matt looked confused when I said that, and I smiled at him.

Cole was quiet for just a second, and then he said. "I'm glad, Jared." It wasn't his usual flamboyant voice. It was his real voice, soft and quiet. "I'm really happy for you."

179

CHAPTER 27

"I GOT the beer!" Matt called as he came in the door.

"It's about time! You missed kick-off." It was Sunday, eight days before Christmas. We had been looking forward to this day for weeks, when our two favorite teams would be playing each other again.

"Anybody score yet?"

"No, but it's only a matter of time before the Broncos pound your pansyass Chiefs into the ground."

He laughed. "We'll see, Jarhead! Loser buys dinner."

It was a close game. We had a blast, harassing each other as first one team took the lead and then the other. With two seconds left, the Broncos were up by one point. The Chiefs were lining up for a field goal. If they missed it, I won. If they made it, he did. It's the folly of sports fans everywhere that we think we can affect the game from our living room. I was yelling, "Miss it! Miss it!" Matt had a white knuckle grip on the coffee table in front of him.

The kick was good. I groaned. Matt let out a victorious whoop and turned and pounced on me from the other end of the couch. It was embarrassing how quickly he could pin me. He grabbed my face and kissed me. Not a romantic kiss, but a big, loud, triumphant smack on my lips, and then pulled back to look at me with a huge smile on his face.

"So what are you buying me for dinner?"

"A Lean Cuisine! You're heavy!"

The phone rang, and I reached over my head to grab it off the side table behind me.

"Hello?" He hadn't moved off of me but had moved down. He had my shirt pulled up and was trying to distract me by kissing his way down my stomach.

"Matt?" a woman's voice asked.

"No, this is Jared."

"Jared? Do I have the wrong number? I'm trying to reach Matt Richards. He told me this was his new number."

He was pushing my sweats lower, and his lips were at the top of my patch of hair. The attempt to distract me was proven successful when I said, "He's on, hang here." He started laughing against my stomach as I handed him the phone.

But the happy look left his face pretty fast once he started talking. I figured out right away that it was his mother and was surprised that he had given them my number. Then I realized he didn't really live at the apartment anymore, so maybe it made sense.

He was sitting up now. "No, Mom, I wish you wouldn't. We're really busy right now. It's just not a good time." Oh shit. I knew by the look he was giving me that his feelings were the same. "Are you renting a car, or do you need me to pick you up?" He put his elbows on his knees and his head in his hands. The remainder of the conversation was nothing but one word answers on his end. "Yes. Yes. Right. Okay. Bye." He dropped the phone, and his head fell almost to the level of his knees.

"Fuck, Jared. This is bad."

Despite his obvious distress, I found that I wasn't too worried about any of it. It would only be for a few days, and then we would be back to normal. And, lately, "normal" for us was unbelievably good. Now that we weren't fighting anymore, everything felt perfect. Nothing could darken my mood much. So my voice was light as I asked, "They're coming to visit?"

"Yes."

"For Christmas?"

"Yes."

"When do they get here?"

"The day after tomorrow."

"How long will they be here?"

"A week."

Neither of us spoke for a minute, but finally I said, as gently as I could, "You don't want them to know, do you?"

"I'm sorry." It came out a whisper.

"After all that shit you gave me about being willing to face people?" But I said it teasingly. I knew what his father was like. I knew how hard it would be for him. I couldn't be mad at him for wanting to avoid it.

"I know," he said quietly.

"Your Dad's gonna totally ruin Christmas." I was still teasing, trying to cheer him up.

"I *know*." I was happy to hear that it seemed to be working.

"And Lizzy is going to blow a fucking gasket."

"I KNOW!" There was at least a hint of laughter in his voice now.

But he still hadn't looked at me. I got down on my knees in

front of him and put my hands on his shoulders. I waited for him to look up at me and smiled at him.

"It's okay," I told him.

He shook his head. "It's not okay. I'm being a hypocrite. Why aren't you pissed at me?"

"Because your Dad's an angry, belligerent, antagonistic asshole."

He laughed just a little. "First time I've ever had reason to be happy about that."

I rubbed the top of his head playfully. "Cheer up. It's not so bad. It sucks that we can't spend Christmas together. And I'll hate not seeing you for a week. But we'll get through this. It'll be fine."

Finally, he relaxed and even smiled a little. "You're really okay with this?"

"I promise."

He pulled me against him tight enough to take my breath away.

"Thank you."

I turned and kissed his cheek and then pulled back so I could look at him.

"I assume you're going to stay at the apartment while they're here?" His lease wasn't up yet, and although it sucked that he still had to pay the rent, it was definitely going to make things easier.

"I'll have to. The motel they use is right across the street. I don't know what to do about the phone, though. I gave them this number. But if they try to call me from the motel...."

"I'll forward the phone to your old number." It wasn't like anybody ever called for me anyway.

I was thinking about the fact that we only had two nights

183

together before we would be sleeping alone again for a week. "You wait here," I told him. I went back to the bedroom and got the lube and then came back and knelt again in front of him, between his knees. He was looking at me with one eyebrow up and half a grin on his face.

"What are you up to?"

I pushed him back on the couch and started to undo his pants. "I thought I'd give you a reason to hurry home."

"You think I don't already have a reason?" he asked with some amusement. But he lifted his hips and let me slide his pants off.

I just smiled at him. "Now you'll have two." I pulled him toward me, so that his ass was almost starting to hang off of the couch. Always, I had to start at the amazing, alluring trail of hair leading down from his navel, kissing it and tasting it. His hands were immediately tangled in my curls. "Have you always had a hair fetish?" I asked him without looking up.

"No." He pulled on it a little, playfully. "Only with you."

That made me smile, and I ran my tongue again up that trail and then started to work my way back down.

"I should ask you the same question," he said teasingly.

Only half of my brain was thinking about his words. I was thinking about the close-cropped hair on his head. "What are you talking about? You don't have any hair."

He laughed, sort of a low rumble that caused his stomach to tremble beneath me. Then one hand tugged on my hair, pulling my face away from him, and his other hand moved to cover his stomach from his navel to his crotch. Covering that beautiful trail of hair.

"Hey!"

I looked up to see him grinning wolfishly down at me. "*Now* do you know what I'm talking about?"

That made me laugh, and I pushed his hand away and kissed him there again. "Ever since our first camping trip. Do you remember me talking in my sleep?"

"About mountain biking."

"Right," I said sarcastically.

"You said something about 'follow the trail'."

"Right," I said again and traced my finger down it.

He laughed again. "I thought you were acting funny that morning."

"I woke up with such a hard on for you, I had to jack off in the tent before I could face you."

He moaned when I said that, and his erection, which had been lying against my cheek as I kissed him, jumped against me. When I looked up, he was giving me a wicked, sexy grin. "*That* is hot," he said huskily. "I have a sudden urge to pitch a tent in the back yard tonight."

I laughed and then put my tongue on the base of his cock and ran it all the way up his shaft. His eyes drifted closed, and I felt a shudder go through him. I did it again, and his hips lifted toward me as I pulled away. His eyes opened again, and he watched me as I teased my tongue over his slit and then took him in my mouth. He groaned. His fingers clenched in my hair, but he didn't push. He never pushed—until he came. Then he would lose his iron control a little bit, and I loved that I could do that to him.

I grabbed the base of his cock and started rubbing my thumb down his perineum. I had been slowly working my way toward his hole over the last few weeks, and he had finally stopped tensing up every time and had even started to enjoy it the last couple of times. This time, he did tense up again, but only for a second, before he relaxed again. I increased the pressure, heard him groan, and felt him pushing against me.

I quickly uncapped the lube and spread a little on my fingers.

"You can tell me to stop at any time," I told him, and I started to suck him again before he could respond. Then, very gently, I started to rub one finger up and down the crack of his ass. Light pressure, no penetration, just slowly rubbing from his balls down past his hole and then back again. At first, he started to tense up again. I kept moving up and down, up and down, still sucking at the same time, just letting repetition soften him up. After a few passes, he relaxed again. A couple more passes, and I heard his breathing start to change, and soon after that, the rhythm of my finger rubbing him had him moaning and moving his hips a little to prolong the contact to the best spots. "Doing okay?" I asked quietly.

"Yeeeesssss." It came out a long moan.

I started circling my finger around his rim and then applied the slightest bit of pressure against his hole. He responded beautifully, moaning and pushing down against my hand. I slipped one finger inside of him and heard his breath hiss out between his teeth. Very slowly, I moved in and out, in and out. He was making soft whimpering sounds now, pushing toward me, his fingers tight in my hair. I reached just a bit and brushed my finger on the bunch of nerves I had been carefully avoiding so far.

His reaction was almost enough to make me come. He bucked underneath me, his hands pulling hard on my hair, and gasped out, "Holy fuck!"

I pulled back away from it again. "You didn't know about that?"

"No." And that, too, was a moan. I reached and touched it again, just barely, just to see him writhing at the unexpected pleasure of it, just to hear the low whimper in his voice. Then I continued with the gentle in and out, in and out.

"Do you want more?" I asked. I didn't look up at him, just went back to sucking him as soon as the question was out of my mouth.

"No." It was sort of a whimper. I kept sucking, kept my finger moving slowly in and out, and then a second later, in barely a whisper, he said, "Yes."

I slid a second finger in, and he moaned again, pushing against me so that my fingers went in faster than before. Two or three strokes, in and out, and then I reached up for his prostate. I felt him jump, heard him gasp out, "Jesus Christ, that's amazing." And then suddenly he was pushing me away, pushing me hard onto my back on the floor, pulling my sweats and boxers off of me frantically. He lay down on top of me, and I felt his hand between my legs, his fingers pushing against me.

"Tell me how. I want to do it to you."

"Lube!" I managed to squeak out, just as he started to push in.

He laughed shakily, sat up and put some on his fingers, and then was back on top of me, his eyes intense on mine. "Tell me."

"It kind of feels like a lump on the front wall. You'll know." And then his fingers were sliding into me, and I couldn't talk any more. My hips rose to meet him. My back arched, my eyes closed. His fingers were moving torturously slow, in and out. After all of that time sucking him and teasing him, I was ready to explode.

I started to stroke my own erection with one hand and his with the other, but he pulled away. "Too close," he whispered, and then his fingers found what they had been searching for. That incredible shock of pleasure hit me. I groaned and arched against him and heard him groan in response. I opened my eyes and looked up at him. His eyes looked greener than usual, heavy-lidded, sensual and unbelievably sexy, and he was smiling at me a little.

"God, I love to watch you," he said, and then he touched it again.

187

"Is this what you feel," he whispered as he touched it a third time. "Is this what you feel when I'm inside of you?"

I couldn't possibly formulate a rational response at that moment. All I managed was some kind of whimper. He didn't seem to mind.

"Jared." His cheeks were bright red, but he still said, "I really want to fuck you right now."

Just hearing him say those words was almost enough to make me come. I managed to say, "I thought you'd never ask." He smiled, sat up, and started digging through the drawer in the coffee table, looking for a condom. Funny how we seemed to have them stashed all over the house now. I started to turn over, but he stopped me.

"I want to see you."

He hooked one of my knees in his elbow. I felt the pressure of his cock against me, and then slowly, very slowly, he pushed in deep, watching my face the entire time. The intensity of his gaze always unnerved me. I closed my eyes and relaxed into that tight, full feeling of having him crammed into me. That gentle friction, moving in and out. He was going so slow, but I was peaking fast. Part of me wanted him to tease forever, but part of me felt like I had to come soon or I'd lose my mind. He pushed my leg up onto his shoulder and then used that hand to start stroking my cock while he thrust in and out. Jesus, when did he get so good at this?

"Jared," he said softly, "I want to be where you are." He was still thrusting, still stroking. "I want to know what you're feeling right now. I want to know what it's like to have you inside of me." His words were definitely pushing me over the edge. I was trying to find something to hang onto, and my hands found the legs of the coffee table. His thrusting and the stroking were both speeding up. "Oh Jesus, Jared." I opened my eyes then, looked into his, and saw surprise and confusion and a whole lot of raw desire there. "I think I really want you to fuck me."

The thought of him on his hands and knees in front of me popped into my mind, and that was it. Everything exploded. I was coming, and so was he, and before the quaking had even stopped, his arms were around me, and he was kissing me. "Well," he said quietly, his lips brushing mine, "maybe next time."

"NEXT time" turned out to be the next night. I was dozing on the couch when he got home from work.

He smiled down at me. "Bed time," he said before pulling me off of the couch and pushing me toward the bedroom. I was still half asleep. I got undressed, got into bed. But instead of getting in behind me and wrapping around me like he normally did, he got into bed on the other side and slid over so that his back was against my stomach.

I drowsily wrapped my arm around him, slid my hand down, and discovered that he was completely naked. I started to wake up a little more then.

"Hope you're not too tired," he said lightly, and then he took my hand and placed a little jar of scented massage oil into it.

Suddenly I was wide awake, and my cock was about to explode just at the thought of what his words meant.

"Are you sure? You don't have to."

"Shut up, Jared." He rolled onto his stomach. "I'm sure. I'm still nervous as hell, but I'm sure."

"Maybe you should be on top. Then you'll have more control."

He thought about it for a second but then shook his head.

"Okay." I wiggled out of my boxers and then sat across his ass. He immediately tensed underneath me. "Just relax. I'm not going to do anything yet."

189

I poured the oil into my hands and started to massage him. I started on his shoulders, which were so big and tense that I feared my hands would be tired before I got any further. But I kept rubbing. Squeezing his shoulders and then rubbing along his biceps, then up and down his back, until he finally started to unwind. Slowly, the tension began to leave him. Still I rubbed, feeling the smooth muscles loosen under my fingers. His body was so beautiful and perfect and strong, and I still couldn't quite believe that he was really mine. I don't know how long I massaged him. My hands were starting to burn, but he was so relaxed that I actually thought he might be sleeping.

I moved down, and knelt between his legs. He tensed a little when I touched his ass but only for a second, and then he made an obvious effort to relax again. I rubbed his legs a little, although I found the sensation of the hairs and the oil against my hands a little strange. Then I slowly moved back up. I poured more oil onto my hands, rubbed some on my cock so I wouldn't have to stop later.

For a minute, I just looked at him, that amazing body glistening from the oil. He was just lying there, hard muscle and smooth, tan skin, legs spread wide, looking unbelievably sexy, waiting for me to fuck him. It made me a little giddy.

He turned his head a little and looked back at me, one eyebrow up.

"Jesus, Matt, I think I could come just looking at you."

He laughed a little and turned back into the pillow, so his voice was a little muffled, but I could still hear the laughter in it when he said, "You better not."

I leaned down over him so that most of my weight was against his back. My cock, which was definitely wide awake and wondering when the party was really going to get started, was wedged down along his crack, pointing toward his scrotum. He barely flinched at all when I put my fingers against his rim and started rubbing gently, just as I had done the night before.

He slid one hand underneath his hips to stroke himself and arched against my hand. I rubbed around his rim while he pumped and heard his breathing becoming frantic. I increased the pressure a little. He was straining hard against me. I pushed in just the tiniest bit and then pulled back out.

"Jared." He sounded frantic. "Please don't tease me."

I slid two fingers into him, and I swear the timbre of his moans dropped an octave.

"Jesus, I still can't believe how good that feels."

I was going faster than I had the night before, moving my fingers in and out, biting a little at his shoulders. He was pushing his ass up into me, gasping and whimpering, and it was making me crazy. I was dying to finally fuck him, thinking that if I had to wait much longer, I wouldn't even make it past penetration before I came. And like he was reading my mind, he suddenly said, "Now, Jared."

I kept my fingers moving in and out while I moved myself into position. Then, as smoothly as I could manage in my extremely aroused state, I pulled out my fingers and slid my cock in without breaking rhythm. It worked well. I was all the way in before he realized and tensed back up. This time, I didn't think it was an objection, just reflex. I froze, waiting for it to pass. "Are you in pain?"

A heartbeat, and then, "No. Not pain."

"Good." I used the hand that wasn't propping me up to gently rub his shoulders some more. "I know it feels strange right now. I know it feels like there's no room for me, but there is. Just try to relax like you were a minute ago." He took a couple of deep breaths, and then I felt him relax around me. "Good." Still, I didn't move, although it was one of the hardest things I had ever done. "Tell me when you're ready." I knew exactly how, after a few seconds, that first feeling of fullness and discomfort and slight pain would start to feel like something much better.

191

I kissed the back of his neck and felt him squirming a little under me, trying to accommodate me. Then his breath caught. He let out a soft moan. Then his whole body seemed to relax a little more, and he pushed his ass up against me.

That was good enough for me. Very slowly, I started to move. Only two or three strokes and he was with me, panting underneath me, arching his back against me. I knew I wouldn't last much longer. I slid my hand underneath him. His hand was still there, although it wasn't moving. I pushed it away and grabbed his cock, started to pump it in time with my thrusts. He lifted his hips up off the bed, which gave my hand more room to work and allowed me to penetrate a little deeper at the same time.

"Oh Jesus, Jared." It was almost a sob. "Oh Jesus, I can't...."

"Can't what?"

He didn't answer, just shook his head.

"What's wrong?"

Nothing *seemed* to be wrong. He was definitely pushing against me, breathing hard, his erection thrusting in and out of my hand as I pushed in and out of him, and I knew he had to be close.

"It's too much," he managed to gasp out.

"Do you want me to stop?"

"Fuck, *no!*"

Thank goodness for that. I wasn't really sure I could have stopped if he had said yes. I was speeding up now, both my thrusts and my hand pumping on him. "Stop fighting it, Matt," I said softly. "Just let go." And amazingly, he did. He went rigid and made a low, guttural cry into the pillows. He tightened around me, his whole body clenched and shaking underneath me, and I came, too, hanging onto him as tight as I could and hoping I didn't actually leave teeth marks in his shoulder.

For a minute, we stayed that way, me on top of him but no longer inside of him, both of us breathing hard and trembling from the strength of our orgasms. And then he suddenly pulled away from me, turned around, and grabbed me. He rolled me so that he was on top of me and crushed me hard against him. He was still shaking.

I ran my hands up and down his back, feeling the tremors finally die away. We stayed like that for a while, just holding each other and running our hands over each other and letting our breathing get back to normal. He kissed my neck a little, but he didn't say anything, and the longer we went without talking, the more I worried about it.

"Matt, are you okay?" I finally asked.

He laughed shakily. "Are you serious?"

"Yes." I pulled back, grabbed his head and pulled him away from my neck so I could look into his eyes. "I'm serious. I want to know if you're okay with what just happened."

He smiled down at me, and I didn't see any shame or regret in his eyes. He looked tired and sated and completely at ease. "Jared, I am somewhere way beyond 'okay'." He kissed me and pulled my hair so he could kiss my neck. "That was amazing. Although...."

That made me worry all over again. "What?"

"The aftershock is kind of strange."

I relaxed again in his arms and laughed a little. "I know."

"I feel sort of—I don't know. *Soft*."

"I know what you mean."

"It feels that way for you?"

"I always feel like my legs aren't quite attached right anymore. Like they're somehow loose in my hips. Like I'm a Barbie and somebody pulled my legs off—"

"No!" he growled fiercely into my ear, his hand pulling hard on my hair. "Not a Barbie!"

"Okay." I laughed, surprised at his response. "Ken, then."

He relaxed a little, but it felt forced, and when he looked down at me, he looked troubled. "You could pass for Ken. Long-hair, hippie Ken." His hands pulled on my curls again, but not as hard this time.

I could tell he was trying to joke, but it didn't quite come out right, and suddenly it wasn't funny anymore. "What is it, Matt? Do you think it makes me a girl if you fuck me?"

He sighed and flopped down on his back next to me and stared up at the ceiling. "No. Not a girl."

"But less of a man?"

He didn't answer, which of course was an answer in and of itself. I tried not be bothered by it. After all, I had lost my virginity fifteen years earlier. Fifteen years and a half-dozen different relationships in that time to explore the dynamics of top or bottom. In most cases, it hadn't mattered, but in some, it definitely had. I knew that it could become a power issue, and I tried to be grateful that he was being cautious of it. Still....

"Jared?" He was on his side now, facing me, his head propped up on his hand. "Are you mad?"

"I'm not sure yet," I answered honestly.

He pulled me back into his arms. "Please don't be. It's not even so much that I think of you that way, as that I worry that you'll think that I think of you that way and you'll resent me for it. Does that make sense?" I was trying to unravel that, but he didn't give me time to answer. "Anyway, I feel better about it now." And it was true that he didn't look troubled anymore at all and his voice sounded determined. "I feel better about what just happened than about the other way."

I still wasn't sure it made much sense to me, but so what? We had been together just over a month. Not long at all for a guy to go from insisting he was straight to where we were now. We had all the time in the world to make him more comfortable. And in the meantime, he preferred bottom? I'd have to be an idiot to object to that.

"Jared, are you okay?" he asked.

I smiled up at him and repeated his own words back to him. "Matt, I am somewhere way beyond 'okay'."

"Good." He kissed me then, and it was slow and deep and passionate, and his hands were wandering down my body in a very familiar way, and I was surprised to feel that he was growing hard again already against my leg.

I laughed. "Already? I'm not sure I'm capable."

"Sometimes," he whispered jokingly into my ear, "you just don't know when to shut up."

He rolled back on top of me, lining us up the way he liked to do, and reached down to wrap his hands around both of us. He was fully erect again, and I was getting there. He was kissing me again, and his strokes were slow and deliberate. I wrapped one arm around him, put my other hand on top of his as it moved on us, closed my eyes, and gave up to the sensation of what he was doing. Fucking him had been incredible, but this was something else entirely. Sexually, maybe it was less, but emotionally, I knew it was more. I knew he was telling me something. It was in the slowness of his movements, the way he gripped me tight against him, the gentleness of his tongue running over my lips, the way he whispered my name.

I was still amazed that I could make him this way.

Nothing else mattered. Not his parents. Not having to spend a week apart. Not even Barbie and Ken.

CHAPTER 28

Two days before Christmas, Lizzy and I were working in the shop. Brian was working on selling it, but until then, it was still ours. I hadn't seen Matt for four days. My house felt terribly empty, but knowing it was temporary made it bearable. I had been spending a lot of time at Brian and Lizzy's and had even done one night of babysitting with little James.

Lizzy was counting out change and talking about her favorite topic, my hair.

"Jarhead, you can't teach like that. What will the kids think?"

"That I'm hip."

"You are not hip. You're scruffy. Not the same thing."

"I thought girls liked scruffy guys."

"Oh?" She grinned at me playfully. "Are you trying to attract girls now? Is there something you're not telling me?" I tried to throw a pencil at her but missed by a mile.

Matt walked in at that moment, looking exhausted.

"Hey, Matt, I'm trying to convince Jared to cut his hair."

He didn't even acknowledge her but walked up to me and said quietly, "Can we go in back for a minute?"

I was surprised but said, "Sure."

We went in the back room. He sat down on the edge of Lizzy's desk, looking down at the floor, and didn't say anything. Sitting on the desk, he was shorter than me, and all I could see was the top of his head. I could tell by looking at him that he was wound up tight. I waited for him to say something and finally realized he wasn't going to.

"How's it going with your parents?"

"Fabulous." His voice was low and tight, full of sarcasm and anger. He didn't look up and didn't seem inclined to say anything else. The silence stretched on. It felt like he was getting ready to share bad news with me, and I tried to keep my pulse from racing.

"What's wrong?"

"I just wanted to see you."

That made me relax a little, but I knew there was something else going on. "That's all?"

He nodded but didn't say anything, and he was still staring down at the floor.

I walked closer, and he tensed up a little, like he might bolt if I made any sudden movements. "Matt, look at me."

It took him a second, like he had to work up his nerve, but when he glanced up at me, I saw it in his eyes. He was barely holding himself together. Coming to me hadn't been a whim. It had been an act of desperation. He didn't just *want* to see me; at that moment, he actually *needed* me, although he could never have said it. He looked sad and terrified and lost. I could tell he was embarrassed for me to see him this way but desperate for me to help him somehow.

I went to him, put my arms around him, and he grabbed on to me like he was drowning and buried his face in my shoulder. He was shaking, his breathing ragged, and I thought he might be crying

197

but trying hard not to. At that moment, I hated Joseph more than I ever had before. I hated that he could break Matt, who was usually so strong and confident, in only a few short days. I don't know how long we stood like that—several minutes at least. I just held him, rubbing his back and shoulders a little, making calming sounds until his breathing was steady again, and he finally relaxed.

"I'm sorry, Jared," he whispered.

"Shhh. Don't be silly. You have nothing to apologize for." I kissed the top of his head. "What happened?"

"Nothing, really. I'm just losing my fucking mind." He laughed, but it was harsh and humorless. "I can't stand it. I can't stand *him*." He took a couple of deep breaths, and then said, in something closer to his normal voice, "I miss you. I hate that we have to be apart right now."

"Me too. Why don't you come over tonight? They don't have to know."

"I'm on nights this week."

So he was working nights and spending the days with his parents and probably barely sleeping in the meantime. That explained a lot about his present state of mind.

He pulled back, stood up, and turned away from me. Even with his back to me, I could see him putting himself back together, wiping his eyes, standing straighter, squaring his shoulders, putting on that carefully controlled, guarded expression. "He's drinking, Jared. A lot. And he never knows when to keep his mouth shut. This is the worst it's ever been."

Just then, Lizzy poked her head around the corner. "Can I come in?" she asked quietly. "I'm sorry to interrupt, but I need to get into the safe."

Matt took a deep breath and then turned around. He was still tense, but he had most of his usual confidence back. To anybody else, he probably looked as calm and in control as ever. But I could still see the anger and sadness in his eyes. "It's okay, Lizzy."

She headed for the safe but watched him out of the corner of her eye the whole time. She got what she needed out of the safe and started out but then stopped and turned to him.

"How bad is it, Matt?"

He shrugged. "Pretty bad."

She thought about it for a minute, and then said, "Why don't you all come to dinner on Christmas?"

"No." He shook his head. "I couldn't do that to you. Not after the way he behaved last time."

She walked over to him and put a hand on his arm, looking way up into his eyes. "Matt, you're family now. You should be with *us* on Christmas. And if that means we have to put up with your father, then we will."

He looked at the floor, then glanced at me, and then at her. "He doesn't know...."

"I figured as much. We'll be careful."

"Really?" He sounded hopeful.

"Really."

He smiled and hugged her, much more gently than he ever hugged me. She looked so tiny in his arms. "Thanks, Lizzy." She started to head back out, but he said, "Oh, Lizzy, one more thing?"

"Yes."

"Jared can't cut his hair. I wouldn't have anything to hang on to. It gives me good leverage."

I had never seen Lizzy turn quite so red so fast. I knew I was blushing too. Matt laughed at us both. And hearing his laugh at that moment was worth all the embarrassment in the world.

I WAS in the kitchen with Mom and Lizzy when Matt and his parents arrived on Christmas day. Matt came in immediately and said quietly, "He's drunk. Lizzy, I hope you don't end up regretting this."

Before she could say anything, Lucy came in. She obviously felt awkward after the debacle of their last visit, but she thanked Lizzy for inviting them, and then Brian brought James in, and the three women were immediately talking about sleeping patterns and nursing habits. Matt, Brian, and I cleared out in a hurry.

We made it most of the way through dinner before the shit hit the proverbial fan.

"I'm surprised that there's no snow," Lucy was saying. "I figured we would have a white Christmas in Colorado."

Brian laughed. "We rarely get snow for Christmas. Any that we do get before this generally melts in a day or two. Our heaviest snowfall is usually February or March."

Suddenly, Joseph looked around the table and said, "Don't you have anything to *drink*?"

Lizzy's smile was all innocence. "What would you like? I have iced tea, Sprite, Dr Pepper, milk—"

"No! I'm talking about a *drink*."

"Oh!" She looked genuinely dismayed. "I meant to get some wine to have with dinner, but I got so busy yesterday, and I forgot to go to the liquor store. And of course, they're closed today." She looked around guiltily and giggled a little and shrugged, and she really did come across as somebody who just couldn't quite keep too much in her head at once. "I'm such an airhead, sometimes. Brian's always teasing me about it."

Of course, that wasn't true at all. Nobody would ever accuse Lizzy of being an airhead, least of all Brian. I also knew that there was plenty of alcohol in the house.

"You mean you don't even have any beer?"

"We finished it off on Sunday watching the game," I told him. Also a lie.

"Well, with the way those Cowboys are playing this season, I can understand that." Of course, the Cowboys game hadn't even been shown that week in Colorado, but we didn't say anything.

I was actually glad football had come up—such a nice, safe topic—and I said, "Can you believe Al Davis fired his head coach again already?"

I could tell Matt was wound up too tight to respond, but this was the one topic I could count on Brian for. "Hey," he said, "as long as he keeps being an idiot, the Raiders keep sucking. He's actually my hero."

But Joseph ignored us and moved on to his favorite subject.

"Matt, I still can't figure out why you're not dating anyone. When we were here last summer, we couldn't go anywhere without some young girl giving you her number. You should be playing the field."

"Dad, can we please not discuss this *again*?"

"Why not? You're never going to find the right girl if you don't date a few."

"Joseph, I'm sure you heard that Matt's girlfriend, Cherie, was killed a few weeks ago," Lizzy said, smooth as ever, and Matt looked at her gratefully. "It was very traumatic. I know her death was very hard on him."

"Horse shit! We never even heard about the girl." As if they talked every day. As if Matt would have shared it with his dad even if he had cared for her. "What about that looker we saw yesterday at the pizza place?"

Matt's jaw was clenched tight, his hands gripping each other tight on the table in front of him. "Dad! Enough."

"What? It's a simple question?"

"It's a simple question which you have already asked me a dozen times. The answer is the same. I'm not interested." His voice had that low, controlled tone, which I knew meant he was furious. Joseph either didn't notice or didn't care. I suspected the latter.

"How can you not be interested? If not her, what about that redhead? Your mother wants grandkids, and you're not getting any younger. Are you ever going to stop being so damn selfish and do your duty?"

"Lucy," Mom jumped in suddenly, "didn't you tell me last time you were here that you were planning a trip to Florida?"

"Uh." Lucy was looking very flustered, fidgeting with the scarf around her neck. I think she could sense disaster in the air but couldn't quite figure out which way to dodge. "Yes, that's right. We went to Orlando—"

"I want to know!" Joseph's voice was much louder now. "I want to know how can you go around with this, this—" He was gesturing at me and obviously couldn't think of a word bad enough. "This *pansy*, like it doesn't matter! It's no wonder none of the girls want to date you."

"Joseph, that's enough," Lucy said quietly, but he didn't listen.

"Have you thought about that? Have you thought about what people are going to say about you?"

Lizzy stood up now. "Mr. Richards, I think I'm going to have to ask you to leave now."

"No! I'm not going anywhere! I want to know why my son is

still hanging around with a fucking faggot. Don't you care what people will say?"

"Joseph." My mother stood up, and her voice was sharp enough to cut glass. "That is my son you are talking about, and—"

"I don't give a rat's ass!"

Mom turned around and slammed her way through the swinging door into the living room hard enough to rattle the pictures hanging on the wall. Joseph was standing up now, swaying a little on his feet. Matt hadn't moved an inch. His hands were clenched in front of him, and he was staring straight ahead, which put his gaze somewhere over his mother's head. Lucy had her hands over her face. Brian had the classic deer-in-the-headlights look. Lizzy was still standing with her hands on her hips, glaring at Joseph with murder in her eyes.

Joseph still wasn't done. "You should be ashamed to be seen with him! Don't you know what that could do to your career? Are you so fucking stupid that you can't figure out what people will say?"

"I know what people say, Dad." His voice wasn't as quiet now. He didn't sound angry anymore at all. Just resigned.

"So you know that they're going to assume you're a faggot too?"

"Yes, Dad, I know that."

"They're going to assume you're his boyfriend."

"I know that too."

"They're going to assume that the two of you are fucking each other."

His voice was stronger this time. "I don't care."

"How can you not care?"

And I saw him make the decision. I saw his hands unclench,

his shoulders relax. I reached out to grab him, to tell him to stop, I even started to say, "Don't," but he shook me off. He sat up straight, squared his shoulder, looked right at his dad and said, "Because it's true."

"Oh no." Lucy's voice was a whisper behind her hands, and she put her head down on the table.

Nobody else moved. Nobody else spoke. The silence seemed to go on forever.

Joseph finally said, his voice low and deadly, "Are you telling me—"

"Yes." Matt stood up now, back straight and head up. I couldn't believe how calm and sure he looked, as if, having now set his feet on the path, he had no reason to look back. "I'm telling you that I'm gay. That apartment you saw? The day I took you there was the first time I had been there in weeks. I live with Jared." I would like to say that I was holding my head up, as proud as he seemed to be, but the truth is, I was doing my best to stare straight through the dining room table in case there was a hole underneath it I could climb into.

Another deathly silence, and then Joseph said, "You are not my son."

And Matt actually smiled at that, just a bit. "I don't remember the last time I agreed with you more." Lucy was really crying now. Nobody moved to comfort her. "Here." Matt tossed a set of car keys on the table. "Take your rental car and go home. I'll be going home—to *my home*—with Jared."

Joseph looked like he was about to say something, but he never got the chance.

Suddenly, Mom burst back into the room. "Matt, you need to come. There's something going on."

Matt, Mom, and Brian went first. Joseph and Lucy followed.

Lizzy was still standing in the same position, hands on hips, staring at the empty place where Joseph had been standing. I was in shock. I felt like the whole world had been turned upside down. I was waiting for somebody to jump out and yell, "Surprise, you're on candid camera!" But instead, Lizzy turned to me and said, "Well, that went better than I expected."

And just like that, I was laughing. She came and pulled me out of my chair. "Come on. Let's go see what's going on."

When we got into the living room, nobody was there. The front door was open, and there were people all over the front lawn. At the curb were several police cars with lights flashing. It was dark outside, and the only light came from the red and blue strobes on top of the cars. Matt was talking to Grant, Tyson, and one other cop I didn't know.

"What's going on?" I asked Matt.

"We need to talk."

"Do you have your weapon?" Grant asked him.

"No."

"There must be a spare in one of the trunks." Grant headed off to the cars.

Matt led me over to where Brian, Lizzy, and Mom were standing. Mom had James in her arms. "Somebody broke into my apartment earlier. They broke all the windows and trashed the place. The neighbors noticed the broken window and called the police." He was speaking quickly and quietly. "When they got there and realized it was my place and that I wasn't there, they went to our house." He looked at me as he said this. "And they found the same thing there."

"*What?*"

"Our neighbor heard a commotion and watched out the window and saw Dan Snyder leaving."

"Holy shit."

"When they didn't find either of us at either place, they got worried and called in everybody."

"Why didn't they call you?"

He suddenly looked sheepish. "The battery on my phone is dead, and the charger is at home." By which I knew he meant at my place, where he hadn't been all week. I felt my eyebrows go up, and he gave me the pseudo-smile. "I know. I'm an idiot. I'm going to catch hell for it later. Right now, they want me to go and help with the search." He reached out and grabbed my wrist. "Jared, stay here. Don't go anywhere until you hear from me." Then to the rest of them, "In fact, you should all go inside and lock the doors. If he knew to go to Jared's house, then he might know to come here next." Lizzy's hand flew up to her mouth, and Mom clutched James to her like she thought Dan was going to jump out of the bushes and try to snatch him out of her arms. "I tried to talk them into leaving an officer here, but they don't think I'm right."

Just then, Grant ran back up to Matt. "I found a gun for you. It's in the car. Are you ready to go?"

Matt looked over to where his parents were standing. Joseph had his arms crossed and was staring at the sky, and Lucy was talking quietly to him. They didn't seem to notice the chaos around them. "Give me one minute, Grant."

"Hurry." Grant turned and went back to his car. The other cops were all back in their cars too. Some of them had left already. The ones that remained were just waiting for him.

Matt took a deep breath and then walked over to his parents. His dad turned his back on him and walked away, but Lucy was listening as he started to explain what was going on. Lizzy, Brian, and Mom went up the steps back into the house. I watched until they were inside and then turned back to where Matt was talking to his mom. That's when I saw Dan.

He stepped out of the dark shadows next to the garage. We were three points of a triangle—Dan on one point, me on the second, and Matt with his mom on the third. I saw his hand come up. I saw the gun. It was pointed right at Matt.

Everything was in slow motion. I was running toward Matt, yelling his name. He and Lucy were just turning to face me when I reached them, and that was when I heard the gun go off. Something slammed into me. Matt pushed past me and ran full speed, straight at Dan. Dan squeezed off another shot, but he was obviously thrown off guard by Matt bearing down on him, because the shot went wide. Matt barreled into him in a tackle worthy of the NFL, knocking the gun out of his hand, and had him pinned on the ground in record time.

I was feeling a little wobbly and turned to see that Lucy was hanging on to me. "I'm so glad I'm not the only one he can do that to," I told her.

For some reason, she didn't laugh. She looked scared. "Jared, I think you need to sit down."

And suddenly I realized she wasn't hanging on to me. She was trying to hold me up.

And then I was on the ground.

"Matt!" she yelled. The whole thing had only taken seconds. The cops were just now getting out of their cars and rushing toward us. I saw Matt, who was still holding Dan to the ground, look over at me and his face went white.

"Somebody bring me some fucking cuffs!"

I was trying to stand up when I heard Lucy say, "Jared, hold still." I realized she was sitting on the ground next to me. "Jared, you've been shot. You need to be still." She pulled the scarf from around her neck and held it against my side.

And suddenly, it hurt.

A *lot*!

I heard somebody say, "The ambulance is on the way." And then Matt was next to me, holding my hand and looking down into my face.

"Hang in there, Jared."

"He shot me?"

"Yes." His eyes left mine as he glanced down to where his mom was pushing hard on my side. Then he looked back at me. "There's a lot of blood."

"Rub some dirt on it."

"He's delirious," Lucy said, but Matt shook his head, a tiny hint of a smile in his eyes.

"No. He's not. He's going to be fine. Right, Jared?"

"Yeah. I feel great. What's for dessert?" He squeezed my hand.

Dan was yelling—I couldn't tell what. Cops were all around, and there was so much noise. I could hear Lizzy and mom crying. And now, it was *really* starting to hurt, and I could hear Grant saying, "Stay back. Give them some room."

"It's just like the movies," I said to Matt. Now he started to look concerned. He was obviously re-evaluating his denial that I was delirious. "Jesus Christ, Matt, it hurts."

"Hang on."

I was feeling very light, like I might float up off of the ground. It seemed good that Lucy was holding me down, although I wished she didn't have to make it hurt so much. There seemed to be lights floating around that I couldn't focus on. I heard Lucy say, "He's going into shock."

"Jared." And now Matt sounded scared. "Jared, I love you. Don't you dare die on me."

I tried to put my hand up to touch his face, but I couldn't quite get it there. My vision was starting to fade. "Matt, I think I'm going to faint now."

"No, Jared! Stay with me!"

I didn't hear anything after that.

CHAPTER 29

THE first few times I woke, I was heavily drugged. I was vaguely aware of a parade of faces: one gray-faced doctor and an army of nurses, all interchangeable in their blue scrubs. Lizzy, Brian, Mom, Matt. Lucy? My molasses brain caught on that one, ripples of confusion, before flowing along into oblivion. I was vaguely aware that there were often people in my room I couldn't see. They talked a lot, but only random phrases stuck with me—"replace the window" and "like a nanny"—but I couldn't make any sense of them.

I kept feeling things crawling on me, but nobody seemed to notice. I finally managed to catch one of the nurses and said, "Bugs on my skin."

She patted my hand and said, "It's the Oxycodone."

I heard the words but had no idea what they meant. I was trying to break the sentence down. It was definitely in English.

I fell asleep again before I got any further than that.

THE time finally came when I woke up, and the world made sense again. The fog in my brain had receded and become only a cloudy blotch in my memory. I was relieved that, at that moment, the only person in the room with me was Matt. He was leaning against the wall, looking out the window.

"Oxycodone makes me itch," I said. Well, maybe there was still a little bit of fog left. I wasn't exactly sure why that was the first thing to come out of my mouth.

His head whipped my direction. "What?"

"The painkiller they were giving me. It makes my skin crawl."

He smiled and came to sit on the bed next to me. "That explains a lot. You kept saying 'bugs.'"

"Next time I get shot, tell them I want Vicodin instead."

"I will." But then his face became serious. "You look like hell. How do you feel?"

"Like I need a shower." I was looking around a little more and realized there were flowers everywhere. "Who are all those from?"

"Mostly your students and various members of the Coda Police Department. The school. Mr. Stevens. A lot of them are from people I don't know. You're a hero, you know?"

"Do I get a cape? I want red."

"The way the story is being told, you bravely jumped in front of Mom and me in order to save our lives." His eyes were crinkling at me, and his voice was light. "You took a bullet for us."

"What am I, the secret service? I was just trying to get your attention. I wasn't planning on getting shot."

He smiled. "Your secret's safe with me."

We didn't talk for a minute, and I started thinking about the scene at the table, before the incident in the front yard. Matt had actually told his dad about us.

"Why did you do it?"

211

He must have been thinking about it, too, because he didn't have to ask what I was talking about.

"That day, I just kept thinking about the choices I had made in my life. Some of the hardest ones were decisions I knew he would hate if he knew about them. But they all turned out to be good. First, I decided not to join the military. And I think that was the right choice. Second." He was ticking them off on his fingers as he talked. "I decided a few years ago to quit dating. I've already told you that my life got a lot easier after that. Then, I decided that your friendship was more important to me than what my coworkers were saying. And that turned out to be a good decision. And then when Cherie died, I decided to accept the fact that I wanted to fuck your brains out."

"And *that*," I interjected, "was a *very* wise decision."

He smiled and winked at me. "It was." His face grew serious again. "So we were all sitting there at the table, and he was screaming. And I was thinking about all of those decisions and how they had brought me to this place in my life where I was really, truly happy for the first time ever. So I asked myself, what's the worst he can do to me? And I knew the answer right away—he could disown me. And I wasn't really sure anymore why that seemed like a bad thing. It was like the solution was right there in front of me, and I was just being too fucking stupid to see it." He was looking down at where our hands were clasped together on the bed by my side. "It's actually a relief. I don't have to waste another second of my life trying to make him happy."

"What about your mom?"

He brightened a little. "Once she calmed down, she told me that she had suspected all along." *Funny how that works,* I thought, remembering my conversation with Brian so many years ago. "I can't really say that she's happy about it, but she knows I'm happy. And that means something to her, I think."

"I thought she was here."

212

"She was. She delayed her flight and spent a couple of days here. Turns out with Dad gone, she and Lizzy and your mom are like three peas in a pod."

"She's gone now?"

"She is, but she'll be back." His eyes tightened a little, and he frowned. "She's leaving him. She went home to get her things in order. Lizzy offered to let her live with them for a while. She said she could use help with James anyway."

"Like a nanny," I said quietly to myself, as one piece fell into place.

"Yes." He was smiling again. "She's so excited to have a surrogate grandchild; I think she would leave my dad for James alone."

We were quiet again as I thought about all that he had said.

"Matt, I'm so sorry. You lost your family, all because of me."

He looked at me with alarm. "What? No! You've got it all wrong." He leaned forward on the bed and put his hand on my cheek. "I didn't *lose* my family because of you. I *have* a family because of you."

I leaned into his touch. "I want to go home. When are they letting me go?"

"Tuesday afternoon. I work the two to ten that day, but I'll get it off."

"Don't. Mom or Brian or Lizzy will give me a ride."

"Are you sure you don't mind?"

"I'm sure. I'll be waiting for you when you get home."

"Will you be naked?" he asked with a wicked grin.

I laughed and pushed him off the bed. "Just wait and see."

213

CHAPTER 30

IT TURNED out to be mom who took me home from the hospital. I was surprised to see that the large front window was covered by plywood. I had forgotten that, prior to showing up at Lizzy and Brian's, Dan had ransacked our house.

"They've ordered the glass," Mom told me. "I think Matt said it would be installed next week. We cleaned up inside as well as we could, but you'll probably need to have the carpet in the living room replaced."

When I got inside, I found that the damage wasn't bad at all. I also found that Matt's bookshelf was now in the bedroom and his home gym was taking up most of the dining room. He had apparently moved the last of his stuff into my house while I was in the hospital.

I went to bed early, settled happily into sheets that smelled like him. I was asleep when he got home. I woke up to him sliding into bed behind me. He carefully cuddled up to my back and wrapped himself around me, making sure not to touch the bandage on my side. I settled back against him with a sigh.

"I'm glad you're home," I told him.

"I'm glad *you're* home. I missed this. The whole week my parents were here, I was sleeping at my apartment. And then this past week, you weren't here. This bed seemed awfully big and empty." His hands were wandering, and he started kissing the back of my neck. "Did the doctors say you're healthy enough to resume *all* activities?"

"They said no sex for six months."

He froze until I started laughing. Then, as his lips brushed my neck again, he said, "That's not funny." But I knew he was smiling.

"They said to be careful and make sure we don't disturb the stitches."

"I'll be very gentle."

And he was. He lined us up, the way he always liked, and stroked us off together, very slow and passionate, kissing me deeply right up until the end when he pulled back to watch me come. And although it still surprised me, it was watching me that sent him over the edge, and he said again in my ear, "God, I love to watch you."

Afterward, we lay tangled together in the dark.

"Jared?" His fingers were playing gently in my curls.

"Yes?" I was more than halfway asleep, perfectly warm and content, back in my own bed. With him.

"Say it for me."

"You're heavy."

"No."

"You're a manipulative bastard."

"No." He was laughing.

"You're right."

He gave one hard tug on my hair. "That's not it either."

"I love you?"

He sighed contentedly. "That's the one."

I lay there, hearing his heartbeat in my ear, feeling his fingers moving through my hair, his smooth skin under my fingers, his legs entwined with mine, and I couldn't imagine anything better in the world. I smiled, although he couldn't see it, wrapped my arms tighter around him, and said it again, only really meaning it this time. "I love you."

It had been less than a year since he had first walked through the door of our shop. It was hard to believe my life had changed so much. And looking back, I had to laugh when I realized one simple thing: the whole thing started because of Lizzy's Jeep.

A to Z

Zach Mitchell is stuck in a rut. His college boyfriend left him ten years ago, but Zach still lives in the same apartment, drives the same car, and feeds his ex-boyfriend's ungrateful cat. His Denver business, A to Z Video Rental, is struggling. He has annoying customers, eccentric neighbors, and an unfulfilling romance with his landlord, Tom.

A combat boot-wearing punk with an attitude, Angelo Green was raised in foster homes and has been on his own since he was sixteen; he has never learned to trust or to love. He doesn't do relationships, so when Angelo takes a job at A to Z Video, he decides Zach is strictly off-limits.

Despite their differences, Zach and Angelo quickly become friends, and when Zach's break-up with Tom puts his business on the line, it's Angelo who comes up with a solution. Together with Jared and Matt, their friends from Coda, Colorado, Zach and Angelo will find a way to save A to Z, but will they be able to save each other too?

MARIE SEXTON was always good at the technical aspects of writing but never had any ideas for stories. After graduating from Colorado State University, she worked for eleven years at an OB/GYN clinic. She quit the clinic at about the same time she started reading M/M romances. At some point in the ensuing months, the static in her head cleared, and her first story was born.

Marie lives in Colorado. She's a fan of just about anything that involves muscular young men piling on top of each other. In particular, she loves the Denver Broncos and enjoys going to the games with her husband. Matt and Jared often tag along. Marie has one daughter, two cats, and one dog, all of whom seem bent on destroying what remains of her sanity. She loves them anyway.

Visit Marie's web site at http://www.MarieSexton.net or find her on Facebook.

Try these romances from DREAMSPINNER PRESS

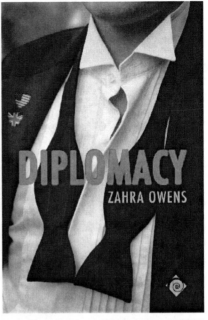

http://www.dreamspinnerpress.com